Baby-sitters' Haunted House

**Other books by
Ann M. Martin**

Rachel Parker, Kindergarten Show-off
Eleven Kids, One Summer
Ma and Pa Dracula
Yours Turly, Shirley
Ten Kids, No Pets
Slam Book
Just a Summer Romance
Missing Since Monday
With You and Without You
Me and Katie (the Pest)
Stage Fright
Inside Out
Bummer Summer

BABY-SITTERS LITTLE SISTER series
THE BABY-SITTERS CLUB mysteries
THE BABY-SITTERS CLUB series

Baby-sitters' Haunted House

Ann M. Martin

AN
APPLE
PAPERBACK

SCHOLASTIC INC.
New York Toronto London Auckland Sydney

The author gratefully acknowledges
Jeanne Betancourt
for her help in
preparing this manuscript.

Cover art by Hodges Soileau

ISBN 0-590-48311-0

12 11 10 9 8 7 6 5 4 3 2 1   5 6 7 8 9/9 0/0

Printed in the U.S.A.   40

First Scholastic printing, June 1995

Summer vacation has just started, and I allready have a two week baby-sitting job. I'm taking care of Karen and Andrew Brewer. Karen is seven years old and Andrew is for. Every day, for two weeks, I'll be finding ways to entertin them — and hopefuly myself. I hadn't expected to start my summer vacatin whith a ful time job!

Claudia

That was the first thing I wrote for my summer English project. I had to write a l-o-n-g composition during vacation. That's because I didn't exactly pass English this year. (You may have noticed that my spelling is pretty bad.) I'm one of those people who have a lot of trouble with writing and reading. Even when I try my best, I'm always making mistakes in spelling, and I'm a very slow reader. Don't feel too sorry for me, though, because I'm talented in anything that has to do with color and design. (Sorry if that sounds conceited, but that's what everyone says about me.) My friends say that I have a unique sense of style, too, and it shows in the way I dress. I have this knack for putting odd pieces of clothing and accessories together in ways that really work. I just don't have a knack for putting letters and words together.

Fortunately, my English teacher, Mrs. Hall, understands my problem. She gave me extra help during the school year. But I still failed. Mrs. Hall was almost as disappointed as I was. So she came up with this idea that if I wrote a very good composition over the summer, maybe I could raise my grade in English to a passing level. When I asked her what I should write about, she said to write about anything

I wanted and that it could be fiction (you know, made up) or nonfiction (something that really happened).

I like fiction, especially mysteries. I'm a big Nancy Drew fan. But since I'm not the type who can imagine stories like that and write them down, I was left with nothing to write about but the truth. So I decided to take notes on what happened to me every day, like a diary. Toward the end of summer I'd read over my diary and use it as an outline for a composition. The day I wrote my first entry in my diary was the day I agreed to sit for Karen and Andrew Brewer.

I got the job through this great club I belong to — the Baby-sitters Club, or BSC. In fact, Karen and Andrew are the stepsister and stepbrother of the BSC's president, Kristy Thomas. Kristy is president partly because she started the club, but mostly because she's the best person for the job. She's smart and organized. She also has a take-charge, no-nonsense kind of personality. Believe me, that's what you need to keep the BSC running smoothly.

Anyway, as I said, I began the notes for my summer writing project with that entry about baby-sitting for Karen and Andrew. As I closed my notebook I was more than a little worried that my composition was going to turn out to be boring with a capital "B." Why would Mrs. Hall — or anyone else for that matter — want to read about me and a couple of kids looking for things to do on hot summer days? It would end up being a boring story about people trying not to be bored.

As it turned out, what happened to me, my friends, and our baby-sitting charges was as exciting as any made-up story, even a Nancy Drew mystery. I could never have imagined that soon we would all be spending two weeks in a *haunted house*.

Claudia

The last week of school before summer vacation went on fourever. And it was hot! The tempratur was over ninty evry day. When the school year was finely over, my freinds and I were jumping out of our swety skins with exsitment. We had all sorts of ideas about how to celabrate. Whitch is what we were talking about at our first Baley-sitters Club meeting of the summer.

Claudia

"I say we start vacation off with a day at the mall," I told Dawn Schafer, Mary Anne Spier, and Shannon Kilbourne. "I need a bunch of art supplies. And some beads for making earrings. Besides, the mall is air-conditioned. What do you say?"

"I'm baby-sitting all day tomorrow," Dawn replied. "For the Prezziosos."

"I'm sitting, too," Mary Anne said.

"Then let's have a sleepover tonight," I suggested. "One with pizzas, ice cream, the works. Guys, this is *vacation*."

"I'm sitting tonight," Shannon said.

"Me, too." Mary Anne, our club secretary, was looking over our baby-sitting schedules in the record book. I'll tell you more about that in a minute. "And Claud, you're scheduled to sit for the Newtons. Actually, we're all pretty booked up this week. Especially you, Kristy."

"Good!" Dawn, Shannon, and I said in unison.

We blamed Kristy for our fuller-than-ever workload during the first week of vacation.

"Why are you guys giving me a hard time?" Kristy asked. "I told you, if we turn down jobs at the beginning of the summer we'll look bad."

"Come on, Kristy," Dawn said. "A day or

two off wouldn't have ruined the club."

"Everyone needs a break," I added. "We've all been studying and taking finals. One of us even has *homework* this summer." I bit into a Twinkie for comfort.

"I'm sure you'll do a good job on the composition, Claud," Mary Anne said. "Don't worry about it." Mary Anne cares a lot about people's feelings and tries to make everyone feel good. But even sweet Mary Anne wanted a break from sitting. "It does seem like we're awfully busy," she told Kristy.

"Look," Kristy said, "you guys elected me president. I'm just carrying out my duties. I know what's best for the club."

After a few seconds of stony silence we started talking again about what we would do with our free time, if we had any.

"The beach," Dawn said. "I'd go into the ocean and not come out until Labor Day."

Out of the corner of my eye I could see Kristy watching the clock. She was determined to start the meeting on time. No slacking off just because it was vacation!

I guess it sounds as if all we do at our meetings is bicker. But it wasn't five-thirty yet, so the meeting hadn't officially started. Besides, everyone was pretty wound up over the last day of school. Anyway, I'd better fill you in on all this Baby-sitters Club stuff.

The idea of the BSC is that we work together to provide a baby-sitting service. We meet three afternoons a week — Monday, Wednesday, and Friday — from five-thirty to six. Our clients know that's when to call to make baby-sitting arrangements for their kids. The BSC always meets in my room. Why? Because I have my own phone line, which means our club calls don't tie up anybody's family phone.

Another feature my room offers is a good supply of junk food. I collect it and share it. No one goes hungry during a BSC meeting, not even Dawn, who's into health food. That's why, while we were complaining about our overstuffed schedules, I was looking for something healthy for Dawn to eat. I found an unopened bag of rice cakes under my bed and handed them to her. "I got these for you," I said. "Though you could just chew on shredded paper and it would taste the same."

"Not to me," Dawn said with a grin. "Thanks, Claud."

"Don't mention it. It's my job as vice-president, right?" Actually, I am vice-president of the BSC. I don't have many official duties, but I take my unofficial ones — such as snack providing — seriously!

I plopped down on the bed next to Dawn and opened a bag of nacho-flavored cheese twists. "I still wish we'd planned a little time off," I told Dawn.

"Me, too," she replied. "Maybe I could have gone back to California for a few days." Dawn's our alternate officer, which means if one of our officers is absent she takes over her job. (Our club has eight members right now, by the way.) But lately she's been *alternating* between California and Stoneybrook. Dawn's father and her brother Jeff live in California, which is where Dawn lived before her parents divorced. Recently, Dawn spent a few months with her father and brother, but now she's back in Stoneybrook where she lives with her mother, her stepfather . . . and his daughter, Mary Anne Spier. The same Mary Anne Spier who's our BSC secretary.

Here's the neat thing. Mary Anne and Dawn were best friends before their parents got married. Now they're sisters, too. In a way, I think that makes things even harder for Dawn. She's torn between her California family and her Stoneybrook family. She loves them both and enjoys the life in both places.

I think if it were up to Mary Anne, she'd vote for Dawn to live with her in Stoneybrook all the time. She really loves being part of a family with a mother, father, and sister in one house. You see, when Mary Anne was a baby, her mother died, so for years and years it was just Mary Anne and her dad. Then came the happy ending: he re-met and fell in love with his old high school sweetheart, who also happened to be Dawn's mother! The rest is history — happy history for Mary Anne.

As I said, Mary Anne is secretary of the BSC. That means she keeps our record book up-to-date. The record book is not to be confused with the BSC notebook. We all write in the notebook about every single sitting job we take. Then we all read the notebook once a week. That way, we keep up on how things are going with the different kids we sit for. No one gives me a hard time about my bad spelling. But writing in the notebook is not one of my favorite things to do.

Mallory Pike (Mal), on the other hand, loves to write in the notebook. She wants to be a children's book author and illustrator someday. So, for Mallory, writing in the BSC notebook is just practice for her career as a writer. Mallory is a terrific baby-sitter. She had a lot of experience taking care of kids before she joined the club. She has seven younger sisters and brothers, including ten-year-old identical triplet boys. Jobs at the Pikes' always require two sitters. (By the way I have only one sibling — my sister Janine who's sixteen.)

Mallory is one of the two junior officers of the BSC. The other is Jessica Ramsey, known as Jessi. They're called junior officers partly because they're young (Jessi and Mallory are eleven while the rest of us BSC members are thirteen), and partly because they aren't allowed to baby-sit at night yet, except for their own brothers and sisters. Jessi and Mal both love sitting and are extremely responsible.

Jessi has an eight-year-old sister, Becca, and an adorable baby brother named Squirt. Jessi is a terrific ballet dancer. She takes lessons in Stamford, which is the city closest to Stoneybrook. Jessi and Mallory are best friends.

My best friend, Stacey McGill, is a *former* member of the BSC. In fact, she's also my *former* best friend. Recently, there was a big fight between Stacey and the BSC, and as a result of that she quit — or was fired, depending on who's telling the story. She and I haven't completely made up, but at least we're talking. No one else in the club is even speaking to her. It's still a big mess, and I'm pretty torn up about it.

Stacey was the treasurer of the club. Dawn, as the alternate officer, has taken over that job.

With Stacey gone, Shannon's been coming to the meetings more often. Shannon and Logan Bruno (he's Mary Anne's boyfriend) are associate members of the BSC. They are both responsible sitters we can call on in a pinch.

Anyway, there we were, still trying to figure out how we could fit a little fun into our overbooked lives, when suddenly Kristy yelled out, "This meeting of the Baby-sitters Club will come to order." I guess it was the second time she'd said it because she sounded a bit angry.

Jessi, Mallory, and Mary Anne said, "Sorry, Kristy," and gave her their full attention. But Dawn, Shannon, and I kept on talking. What finally shut us up was the ringing of the telephone.

"Hello, Baby-sitters Club," Kristy said cheerfully into the phone. She was glaring at us. "Oh, hi, Lisa," she continued. "Yes, we're all glad that school's out. . . . No, we're working just like always. No one's going on vacation for awhile."

Dawn, Shannon, and I groaned — quietly enough so Lisa wouldn't hear, but loudly enough so Kristy would. Jessi and Mallory shot us a Look. I think they were a little shocked at how unprofessional we were acting. Mary Anne looked as if she wanted to groan, but didn't. She would never do something that could hurt Kristy's feelings. Kristy is Mary Anne's other best friend. They've known each other since they were in diapers.

"Two weeks starting tomorrow?" Kristy asked Lisa. "Sure. We'll get right back to you."

Kristy hung up the phone and looked around the room at us. "Lisa and Seth need a sitter for Karen and Andrew for the next two weeks," she said. "Seth's assistant in the workshop broke her wrist. Lisa's going to fill in for her."

I told you that Karen and Andrew are Kristy's stepsiblings. Their father, Watson Brewer, is married to Kristy's mother. I guess this is as good a time as any to tell you about Kristy's big, extended Brewer-Thomas family. When her mother married Watson Brewer, Kristy, her mother, and her three brothers — Charlie (who's seventeen now), Sam (fifteen), and David Michael (seven and a half) — moved into Watson's mansion. (Yes, Watson is rich, *very* rich). Karen and Andrew live with their mother, Lisa, and her second husband, Seth Engle, half the time, and stay with their father and his family the other half. (They switch houses every other month.) There's one more child in this extended family — Emily Michelle Thomas Brewer. She's a sweet two-and-a-half-year-old that Watson and Kristy's mother adopted. We all love to baby-sit for Emily. So does Kristy's grandmother, Nannie, who takes care of Emily while everybody else is working or at school. Nannie lives in the mansion, too.

Anyway, Kristy gets along great with Andrew and Karen. Whenever a baby-sitting job comes up for them, Kristy has first choice.

"Mary Anne," Kristy asked, "am I free to sit for Karen and Andrew?"

"You're booked pretty solid during those two weeks," Mary Anne said. "We'd have to do a lot of switching around."

"Who else could do it?" Kristy asked.

"If Mallory could take Claudia's job Friday morning with the Newtons, Claud could do it," Mary Anne told us.

"It's fine with me," Mal said.

"Then I'll take the job for Karen and Andrew," I said. I guess I was feeling a little guilty about my bad attitude earlier in the meeting. Taking care of Karen and Andrew would be a lot better than going to school every day. At least I was still on a vacation from school.

"Great," said Mary Anne.

The phone rang again. "I'll get it," Dawn said. She picked up the phone, smiled at Kristy, and said cheerfully into the receiver, "Hello, Baby-sitters Club." I guess she was feeling a little guilty, too.

CHAPTER 2

Kristy

I knew you guys wanted a break when school let out, but I was afraid it'd be bad for business if the BSC members turned down jobs. Then after the last meeting I was worried that I'd destroyed the club spirit. Now, I just want to get out of Stoneybrook and have a break myself. You guys were right. We could use a change of scene. How about a seaside vacation in a quiet town?

"So Karen says that Andrew and I should pretend we're animals — only she'll tell us which ones."

While we were waiting for our Wednesday BSC meeting to begin, Claudia was filling us in on her job taking care of my stepbrother and stepsister, Andrew and Karen. They're great kids. I wished I could have taken the job.

Claudia lifted her mattress and retrieved a bag of Tootsie Rolls she'd stashed there.

"What animal did she tell you to be?" I asked.

"A pony," Claudia said. "Only I had to walk backwards on my hands and knees so my ponytail would be . . ."

Dawn and I finished the sentence: ". . . a pony's tail."

"Right," Claudia answered. "And she told Andrew he was a frog. Which of course he loved."

Claudia plopped down on her bed, tore open the bag of Tootsie Rolls, and passed it around. "But here's the best part," she said. "Karen made herself a parrot. A *talking* parrot."

We laughed. It was just like Karen to figure out a game that let her be the only one who could talk! I love how her mind works.

By then Mal and Jessi had arrived and it was time to begin the meeting.

I think Dawn, Shannon, and Claudia were sorry for having behaved so unprofessionally at our last meeting, because everyone quieted down before I even said, "This meeting of the Baby-sitters Club will now come to order." To tell the truth, for one of the first times I can remember, I wasn't really in the mood for a meeting myself. I'd been playing a pickup game of softball with some of the kids on my softball team (the team name is the Krushers and I'm the coach). I was thinking that Claudia had a point. Maybe we all did need a vacation.

The meeting went along in the usual fashion. There were three calls in the first fifteen minutes. We assigned the jobs and called the clients back so they'd know which sitter to expect. Then Lisa Engle, Karen's and Andrew's mother, called.

I answered the phone. By the time I hung up, everybody else was practically jumping out of their skins with curiosity. It had been a long conversation, and they'd only heard my side of it. Which meant they'd heard things such as, "seaside town" and "mansion" and "I'll have to ask Claudia."

"What?" they asked in unison as I hung up the phone.

"Here's the deal," I said. "Friends of Lisa and Seth — people named the Menderses — have just inherited a mansion in Reese, Maine."

"That's an old whaling town on the Atlantic Ocean," Mary Anne said. "I read about it in a travel book. I was — "

"Mary Anne!" Dawn shrieked.

"Sorry," Mary Anne said. "Go ahead, Kristy."

"So," I continued, "Mr. Menders inherited this mansion from an uncle. The thing is, the Menderses don't know if they want to live in it."

"Why wouldn't they want to live in a mansion?" Claudia asked.

"Maybe there are ghosts in it," Dawn teased.

"They're not sure if they want to move out of Boston," I explained. "They have two jobs, four kids, and a life in the big city."

"Reese is a pretty small town," Mary Anne added. "It's one of those resort towns with only a couple of thousand people. But the population doubles or triples in the summer."

"Anyway," I continued, "the Menderses are

going to go there for a long summer vacation. They've invited Seth and Lisa to visit for ten days to help them decide what to do."

"Does that mean Seth and Lisa don't need me to sit?" Claudia asked.

"They're hoping that you'll go with them to take care of the kids. The adults want to be free to explore the area. The Menderses have this idea that they might open a health food store. And since Seth is a carpenter and knows a lot about construction, he can help them evaluate potential store space and tell them how much it would cost to fix it up."

"Didn't you say that the Menderses have four children?" Claud asked. "With Karen and Andrew, that makes *six* kids I'd be taking care of."

"Don't faint yet, Claud," I said. "Lisa thought of that, too. She'd like another sitter to go along to help with the Menders kids."

"I'll go," Dawn said. "I love the idea that the Menderses want to open a health food store. I could help them. I've been in enough of them."

Mary Anne spoke up. "I read all about Reese and I'd love to go there. I mean if Dawn doesn't."

"I'm sorry to disappoint you," I said, "but

since Karen and Andrew are my steps, it seems like I should be the one to go."

Claudia and Dawn shot me nasty looks. I guess they were still angry at me for insisting that we work hard at the beginning of vacation.

Shannon said, "I don't want to go anywhere for the next few weeks. I'll be away at camp for all of August. Count me out."

Mal and Jessi had been quiet through this whole discussion. Finally Mal said, "I'd love to go. I'm used to taking care of lots of kids."

"It'd be so great to get away," Jessi said wistfully.

"You guys," I said. "I'm supposed to call Lisa right back. She needs *one* extra sitter and *five* of us want to go. What am I going to tell her?"

"Well, I don't even know if my parents will let me," Claud said.

I realized that none of us had permission. (Though I was pretty sure I'd get it without any trouble, since I'm related to Karen and Andrew.) "Okay," I told the others. "I'll call Lisa back and tell her we're finding out who can get permission to go. But since whoever goes leaves on Saturday, we better have an answer for Lisa by our Friday meeting."

Kristy

"Let's ask Logan to come to the meeting," Dawn suggested.

When I arrived at Claudia's for the meeting on Friday she greeted me with, "I can go. I've already started packing." All over her room — our BSC meeting room — were piles of clothes, and Claud was dragging her huge suitcase out of the closet. Claudia never goes anywhere without a zillion changes of clothes.

Next, Mary Anne arrived. "Wait until you hear," she said. "Reese is the most amazing place. I'd love to tell the Menderses all about it. They'll want to live there for sure." She was carrying two library books on the history of Maine and a travel guide to New England seaside towns.

Just then Dawn came bounding up the stairs and into Claudia's room. "Great news. My mother said I can go, no problem. Actually, Mary Anne's dad said she can go, too. And you know what I did? I went over to the health food store and asked them how they opened the store, where they buy wholesale . . ." She held up a notebook. "I took notes for the Menderses."

"The sitting job is for the kids," I said crossly. "Not the parents."

Shannon and Logan ran into the room right

22

behind Dawn. Then Mal and Jessi showed up. "We couldn't get permission to go to Reese," Jessi said.

"But we can take over the day jobs of whoever goes," Mal added.

"Great," I told them. "Then I can go. Between Mal and Jessi for my daytime jobs, and Shannon for the night ones, I'll be covered." I reached for the phone. "I'll call Lisa."

Dawn clapped her hand over the phone so I couldn't pick up the receiver. "Not fair," she said. "Kristy, you're the one who said we all had to work. Now *you're* going on vacation?"

"But Karen and Andrew are part of my family," I said. "Besides, it's not a vacation. It's a job sitting for four kids. And I have permission."

"Well I have permission, too," Dawn said.

"Me, too," Mary Anne said.

"Me, three," said Claud.

"I'm the president," I said. "There wouldn't be a Baby-sitters Club without me."

The phone rang. Dawn took her hand away so I could answer it. (I was feeling pretty bad about how I was behaving — extremely bossy and more than a little selfish.)

The caller was Lisa, wanting to know who the second sitter would be. I know Lisa pretty well, so I felt I could be honest with her.

"Lisa," I said, "Mary Anne, Dawn, Claudia, and I all got permission to go. Now we're trying to figure out which one of us will take the job."

"Oh," Lisa said. "That sounds to me as if maybe *all* of you want to go."

"Something like that," I told her.

Lisa was silent for a second, then said, "I wonder if it wouldn't be more fun for the kids, and for the sitters, if all four of you came. It could be a vacation for everyone that way. The mansion is huge, so there's plenty of room. Instead of paying you, you'd get an all-expenses-paid trip to Maine. What do you think?"

I grinned at the others. They were still angry at me for my "I'm-the-president" outburst, and they wouldn't smile back. I couldn't blame them. I'd been pretty obnoxious.

I told Lisa, "I think that's a great idea. Let me talk to the others and I'll call you right back."

When I told everyone Lisa's idea, Dawn, Mary Anne, and Claudia began hugging and hooting. Suddenly Mary Anne stopped and said, "But what about all the baby-sitting jobs we've lined up here?"

"Jessi and I can take a lot of them," Mal said eagerly. "You guys, just leave the BSC to us." They actually looked happy about the idea of getting rid of us. I guess we hadn't been much fun to be around lately.

Logan put an arm around Mary Anne. "I hate the thought of your going away for ten days, Mary Anne," he said. "But I know how much you want to go to Reese. So I'll take over as many of the jobs as I can."

"Me, too," Shannon said. "I could use the money."

The meeting ran overtime, but we managed to come up with a schedule that freed Claudia, Mary Anne, Dawn, and me for a two-week working vacation in Reese, Maine.

We were going to leave the next morning. That was barely enough time for Claudia to pack!

CHAPTER 3

Mary Anne

Saturday Night
11 P.M.

I'm settled in my room in historic Randolph mansion. This is the first entry in the BSC Reese Notebook. Kristy, I thought Watson's mansion was big. This place is gigantic. Even with sixteen people staying here, there's one whole floor we're not using!

Dawn, I didn't want to admit it, but you're right about this place feeling haunted.

On Saturday morning Dawn and I woke up at seven o'clock. We were going to Maine and we still had packing to do. We ran back and forth between each other's rooms with questions such as: "Are you taking your navy stretch pants?" (Dawn to me); "Should I take sneakers *and* sandals?" (me to Dawn); and, "Do you think I should pack my cowboy boots?" (Dawn to me). At one point — actually mid-point between our rooms — we bumped into one another as we asked in unison, "How many T-shirts are you bringing?"

At quarter to ten, Sharon (who's Dawn's mother and my stepmother) dropped us off at the Engles' house. We hugged her good-bye. (We'd said good-bye to my dad earlier.) A van was parked in the driveway. Seth had rented it so he could drive eight of us to Maine. Extra expenses such as this were one of the reasons we weren't getting paid for sitting.

As Sharon drove off, Seth and Lisa came out of their house lugging suitcases.

"Do you want some help?" Dawn asked.

"If you could go out back and collect Andrew and Karen," Lisa said, "we can manage this."

Dawn and I walked around the house to the backyard. We could hear Karen and Andrew discussing the seating arrangements for the trip. "You can sit next to Claudia," Karen said.

"Kristy, too," Andrew said. "I want to sit with Kristy *and* Claudia."

"But I want to sit between Kristy and Mary Anne," Karen told him. "We cannot fit five in a seat."

Andrew looked up and saw us. "Dawn, Kristy, Claudia, *and* Mary Anne," he shouted. "I want to sit next to all of them."

"You cannot, Andrew!" Karen yelled back. "It is impossible!"

Dawn and I exchanged a smile. Karen can be so precocious (that means smart for her age).

"Hi, guys," Dawn said. "Isn't this a perfect day for a trip?"

"We have four baby-sitters," Andrew said as he jumped up and ran over to us. "One — two — three — four."

"Yes," I said. "And you can take turns sitting with each of us during the trip. How about that?"

"Yeah!" Andrew shouted as he ran off to tell his mother the good news.

As soon as we were in the frontyard again, Claudia and Kristy arrived in Charlie's car. Claudia's suitcase was so big and heavy that it took Charlie *and* Kristy to carry it. The rest of us wore ordinary shorts and T-shirts for travelling, but not Claud. She had on a pair of bright blue Lycra biker shorts, a black lacy tank top, a man's white dress shirt, baggy purple and white checked socks, red high-tops, and a pair of big gold hoop earrings with a brightly colored wooden parrot perched on each hoop. She was carrying this humongous, bright yellow, plastic beach bag stuffed with junk food for the trip.

"Hi, everybody," Claudia called out. "I hope we're not late. My parents took ages to say good-bye. You'd think we were going away forever."

Kristy, weighed down with her end of Claudia's suitcase, mumbled, "I wonder where they got that idea. Could it be because you packed everything you own?"

"Claudia," Dawn teased, "we're *visiting* Reese, not moving there."

At ten-thirty we were all finally buckled into the van and ready to begin what should have been a six-hour-plus drive to Reese, Maine. For us, the "plus" ended up being an extra three-and-a-half hours. One hour for lunch at a diner, one hour for getting lost, and one-and-a-half hours for a picnic supper.

Even with my trusty guidebook of historical New England towns and Lisa's detailed road map, we made a wrong turn that detoured us through part of Vermont. I was sort of glad, though, because it meant that on our way to Reese, Maine, we went through charming, historic villages in four New England states: Connecticut, Massachusetts, New Hampshire, *and* Vermont. Before we reached each town I read aloud from the guidebook. So as we were driving through, we already knew about the town's history, current and past industries, tourist attractions, and even the names of the best places to eat and sleep.

I might have gotten a little carried away. Once, as we were zipping along on a highway that bypassed a number of historic towns, Lisa said, "Mary Anne, I think the children might get more out of that book if you stuck to the towns we actually pass through and didn't read about the ones we're not even seeing."

I looked around the van. Next to me, in the middle seat, Kristy and Andrew leaned against one another. They were sound asleep. In the backseat, Claudia and Karen were playing cat's cradle and humming "A Bear Went Over the Mountain." Dawn was listening to her Walkman. I'd pretty much lost my audience anyway.

I was staring out the window and feeling bad about boring everyone to death, when

Seth asked, "Mary Anne, where should we stop for a picnic?"

I flipped to the handy index in the back of the guidebook and looked up state parks. I found one that didn't take us too far out of our way. I was glad we ate our supper picnic style. It gave everybody a chance to run around and burn off some of the excess energy we'd stored up from being in the van all day.

But finding the park, eating, and cleaning up took a lot of time. So it was late when our van passed through the gates of the Randolph estate. Even though it was dark out, we could see the mansion — white and massive — on top of a hill at the end of the winding driveway.

"Wow!" was all I could say. We were amazed by the size of the mansion. It was four stories high, with a six-columned entranceway. Five brick chimneys pierced the cloudy night sky. And there was an authentic widow's walk on the roof.

"Look," Claudia said. "It has a deck on the top. How strange."

"That's a widow's walk," I explained.

"Why is it called that?" Karen asked.

"Because that's where a woman went to watch for her husband's return from long whaling trips. She could get a good view of the ocean from up there."

"Then how come it is not called the 'wife's walk?' " Karen asked.

Before I could answer, Karen came up with the answer herself. "Oh, I know," she said. "Because sometimes the boat sank and the husband drowned in the sea and no one knew yet. So the woman walking up there was a widow, but she did not know it yet. That is sad."

I told you Karen was precocious.

As we tumbled out of the van, Mr. and Mrs. Menders hurried outside to greet us. Behind them I could see the Menders kids standing in the brightly lit front hall of the mansion.

We unloaded our stuff and brought it inside.

Mr. and Mrs. Menders were really glad to see Seth and Lisa. And Karen and Andrew had met the Menders kids before, so they weren't total strangers.

When we'd dropped our luggage in the hall, Mr. Menders said, "Let's all sit around the table in the dining room. We'll have some lemonade and make introductions in there." As we followed the Menders family into the dining room, I thought that they seemed a little lost in the big place.

We took seats at one end of the huge dining room table. (I'm going to stop saying *massive*, *huge*, and *big*. Trust me, everything in this place — except the people — was oversized.) When we had passed around the lemonade, Mr. Menders said, "Why don't we go around the table and introduce ourselves. Say your name and something about yourself. That'll help the sitters get to know the kids and vice versa." I decided that Mr. Menders must be a corporate business type who was used to running meetings.

Jason, who's nine, introduced himself by saying, "I'm Jason. How come if there are four sitters, and there are four of us, and two of us are guys, two of you aren't guys, too?"

Lionel, who's fourteen (and too old to need a sitter) said to his parents, "I'm not sure why we have a gaggle of sitters in the first place. We don't need help to figure out that Reese is a nowhere place to be. I mean, the house is swell, but the town is *nothing*."

"Actually," I began, "Reese was once — "

Dawn kicked me under the table. I realized she was telling me to be quiet. It probably wasn't the best time to begin a historical lecture about Reese.

"We've already discussed this, Lionel," his mother said. "Your father and I think you could use some company during this vacation. The girls are your age. They'll help you meet other kids."

Lionel sighed and said, "Whatever."

My instant assessment of Lionel Menders was: pretentious and unhappy. He may not have needed a baby-sitter, but it was clear to me that he could use some friends, and a change of attitude.

"I think Reese will be lots of fun," ten-year-old Jill said. I noticed that she had moved her chair close to Dawn's. Then I noticed something else: When we arrived, Jill's hair had been in a long braid down her back. Now, her hair was draped loosely over her shoulders, just like Dawn's. She listed her likes and dislikes. Likes: swimming, dressing up, dancing, summer, teenagers. Dislikes: People who act like babies, winter, being bored.

Martha, a seven-year-old, introduced herself by saying her name. Period. OK, she was shy. And being a shy person myself, I could tell that Martha was a little overwhelmed by Karen's bubbly, outgoing personality. I overheard Karen tell her, "We are going to have so much fun. I am great at meeting new people. You will be the most popular person in Reese in no time."

"I don't know," Martha said meekly. "I miss Boston."

Next the baby-sitters and the adults introduced themselves. (I was right about Tom

Menders being a corporate businessman.) When the introductions were finished, Mr. Menders told us, "You'll meet Mr. and Mrs. Cooper in the morning. They'll be making our meals, cleaning up, and generally being helpful."

My friends and I exchanged a glance. A mansion with a caretaker couple! Even if the kids were going to be a challenge, we were going to be taken care of, food-wise and otherwise. We were used to baby-sitting jobs for which we had to do everything.

"Of course," Mrs. Menders said, "since there are so many of us, we'll all be pitching in."

"Of course," Kristy said.

"But when it comes to household matters," Mrs. Menders continued, "the Coopers are in charge."

"Did they come with the mansion?" Kristy asked.

"No," Mr. Menders said, "we've just hired them for the summer. But if we decide to stay, we hope they will, too. They've already proven to be very helpful. They're quite charming and have lived here since they were young."

"Don't forget that little matter of Mrs. Cooper's voice," Lionel put in.

"What?" Dawn asked.

Lionel began speaking in the deep, accented voice of a horror movie narrator. "Mrs. Cooper doesn't ha-ave a vo-oice. She's afflicted with chronic laryngitis. There may be permanent injury to her vocal cords. Ve-ry sta-range."

Lionel put on a menacing expression to match the scary voice he was using.

"Oh, Lionel," Jill said matter-of-factly, "quit it."

"Lionel's always trying out different characters," Jason said by way of explanation. "He's going to be an actor."

"I *am* an actor, my dear boy," Lionel said. "Please, be precise," (Now he was impersonating a rich English gentleman.)

"Well, gang," Mr. Menders said, "it's after ten. Let's set the girls up in the west wing and call it a night. Shall we?"

We carried our luggage (Mr. Menders helped Claudia) up the wide marble staircase and down a long corridor, through a doorway that led to another set of stairs, that led to the hallway of the third floor. We and our charges would occupy eight bedrooms which opened onto this hallway — four on each side. "Okay," Mr. Menders said. "Your first job is to figure out who sleeps where. Our kids will tell you which rooms they've already claimed."

Mary Anne

We did a lot of shuffling around and discussing, but, finally, we settled on the following room assignments.

Facing East	Facing West
Kristy and Andrew	Dawn
bath (connecting)	(connecting door)
Mary Anne	Claudia
Karen and Martha	Jason
(connecting door)	(connecting door)
Jill	Lionel
Bath	Locked door to
	fourth floor stairs

By the time we figured out our room arrangements, Lionel and Jason were already in their rooms with the doors closed. I took Martha and Karen to their room and put them to sleep with a story. When I came back into the hall I saw that Jill was sleepily trailing Dawn. ("I'll go to sleep when you do, Dawn.")

I returned to my own room and looked around. I don't think the third floor of the west wing had been used in a *very* long time. The Coopers had done their best to dust and air everything out. And the beds were made up with fresh sheets. But I had this eerie feeling that I'd gone back in time. As I took in the

details of the room I imagined another girl —
a hundred years earlier — touching the very
same curtain, seeing her reflection in the same
mirror, sleeping in the same bed. A shiver ran
up my spine. I was glad my friends and I had
decided to leave the doors to the hall and between our rooms opened while we unpacked
and got ready for bed.

I studied the headboard of the bed. It was
decorated with a night view of a stormy sea
and a lighthouse. A painted shaft of light
beamed from a lighthouse across the painted
sea.

After I put my clothes away I opened my
casement window and looked out over the
Atlantic Ocean. I could hear its roar and feel
the moist, salty breeze on my face. I noticed
a moving beam of light playing its way over
the ocean. "Kristy," I called. "Come here."

Claudia, Dawn, Kristy, and Jill ran into my
room. We stood at my window watching as
the rough sea was illuminated section by section. "A lighthouse," I explained, "just like
the one painted on my headboard."

"This place feels weird to me," Dawn whispered. "I bet it's haunted."

"Come on, Dawn," I whispered back.
"Don't start. We need a good night's sleep if

we're going to be baby-sitting all day tomorrow."

Just then I felt a furry mass brush against my leg. I shrieked. The furry mass jumped on my bed, arched its back, and hissed at me. It was a black cat with green eyes. I screamed again. This time Claudia, Dawn, and Kristy joined in.

But Jill said, "Oh, there you are, Spooky." She walked toward the cat. "You scared my new friends."

"That's *your* cat?" Dawn asked Jill. (I was still speechless from the fright.)

"Sort of," Jill answered. "It was already here when we came. I guess it was great-uncle Randolph's."

Spooky let Jill pick him up, but his eyes were still trained on me. I love cats. I do. But a black one, slinking out of nowhere?

"Okay, Jill," Dawn said. "It is definitely time for bed. I'll read you a story."

After Dawn, Jill, and Spooky left, I said, "I think I'll close my door."

"Me, too," said Claud as she darted across the hall.

Kristy and I decided to leave the doors between our rooms opened and she returned to her bedroom. I slid between the clean sheets

Mary Anne

and tried to calm down by writing in our Reese Notebook. (The BSC notebook was back in Stoneybrook with Mal and Jessi.)

When I finished my notebook entry and turned off my lamp, I lay in bed listening to the creaks and groans of the mansion. I couldn't close my eyes, much less sleep. I told myself that of course there are creaks and groans. This is a windy night, in a very old house that isn't used to having so many people in it. That's when I saw a flickering light under the door to the hall. At first I thought it must be the beam from the lighthouse, but then I realized the lighthouse didn't shine *in* the house. Flicker. Flicker. There it was again.

I lay stiffly in bed, barely breathing. I was afraid if I stayed alone in my room my heart would *burst* with fright. The doors between my room and Kristy's were still open. I took a deep breath, jumped out of bed, and flew through the bathroom to Kristy's room. She was sitting up in bed, staring at the door to *her* room. Andrew was asleep, so I whispered, "Did you see that?"

Kristy nodded.

"Maybe someone turned on the hall light, and the bulb's nearly burned out, so it's flickering," I suggested.

"It looks like candlelight," Kristy said.

40

"*Ohh — ohh.*" We heard a low ghostly moan in the hall. "*Oh-hh.*"

I grabbed Kristy.

We sat there holding our breath — and each other — as we stared at the door. Then, as suddenly as they had begun, the flickering light went out and the moaning ended.

Silence.

"Do you think Claud and Dawn heard that?" Kristy asked.

"I don't know," I said. "But I'm not going over there to find out."

I spent the night in Kristy's room. By the time I finally fell asleep, I wasn't so sure that I was glad to be in the historic seaside town of Reese, Maine.

CHAPTER 4

Dawn

Sunday
5:00 p.m.

Kristy, I know you're afraid that if we get caught up in this haunted house thing, the Menders kids won't want to move to Reese. But how can we keep the kids from noticing the strange things that are happening in their mansion?

By the way, everyone, keep an eye on Georgio. I don't trust him.

"**G**uys," Kristy said, "if this is such a big house, why are we all crowded into one little bathroom?"

It was seven-thirty on our first morning in Reese, and Kristy, Claud, Mary Anne, and I were brushing our teeth in what was probably the only small room in the mansion — the bathroom between Kristy's and Mary Anne's rooms.

As I brushed my teeth, my elbow caught Kristy in the neck. "Sorry," I gurgled.

"There *is* another bathroom right down the hall," Kristy commented.

"Claud and I heard and saw some pretty weird things last night — " Rinse. Rinse. Spit. Spit. " — in that hall," I said.

In the mirror I saw a look pass between Mary Anne and Kristy. I figured they'd seen and heard some pretty weird things, too. Then we were all talking at once, comparing notes on the ghost.

"Maybe it was our imaginations," Mary Anne said. "You know, because we're in a strange place and everything."

"But we all imagined the *same thing*," I replied. "That's called 'evidence,' not 'imagination.' "

A sleepy voice accompanied a knock on the

bathroom door. "Dawn, are you in there?"

It was Jill. Kristy put a finger to her lips as we exchanged a look silently agreeing not to talk about ghostly matters in front of the Menders kids.

"I'll be right out, Jill," I said.

"What are you going to wear today, Dawn?" Jill asked.

We stifled giggles.

"Shorts and a T-shirt," I answered. "Over my bathing suit. See you at breakfast."

Breakfast was set up on the side veranda, a huge wooden-pillared porch that ran along the side of the house. It was a perfect, clear-skied, warm summer day. The mansion and its grounds were even more impressive in daylight than at night. And *much* less scary.

Cereals, bananas, fresh strawberries, yogurt, juice, and milk were laid out on a sideboard. We served ourselves and sat down around a big wooden table. When Mrs. Cooper appeared with a basket of homemade blueberry muffins, Mrs. Menders introduced her to us. Mrs. Cooper was younger than I expected — probably about my mother's age — and very pretty, with straight dark hair pulled back in a bun. But Lionel was right, she didn't talk. She had a nice smile, though.

As I ate a bowl of fresh strawberries and

Dawn

yogurt, I looked out at the beautiful estate gardens and the ocean beyond. I was thinking about the ghostly apparition of the night before and wondering what ghosts did during the day. Suddenly a deep, ominous voice murmured in my ear, "Sleep well last night, my pretty?"

I shrieked and practically jumped out of my skin.

"Lionel!" his mother said sharply, "That is *not* funny."

Lionel looked around at us sitters and asked in his horror-movie voice, "Ev-very-one get a go-od night's sleep?"

"Just eat your breakfast, Lionel," Mr. Menders said. "You kids can go to the beach today, if you want. The Coopers will pack you a picnic lunch. Tonight we'll have a cookout. And, Lionel, behave yourself."

"Yes, sir. Right, sir." (That was Lionel as a soldier.) Lionel was as annoying with his so-called acting as my brother Jeff is with his so-called comedy routines.

Fortunately, all the kids agreed that they wanted to go to the beach. (Lionel: "I'll go along. If anybody is anybody around here they'll probably be there." Jason: "Sure. Why not?" Jill: "Is that what you're going to do, Dawn?" Martha: "Okay. I guess." Karen:

45

Dawn

"Great. There'll be lots of kids for Martha to meet at the beach." Andrew: "Can I look for frogs? Can I?")

The adults made sure we knew the way to the beach, and gave us some beach rules to follow with their kids. We decided that, for the morning, at least, Claud and I would be responsible for Karen, Martha, and — since she was practically glued to me anyway — Jill. Kristy and Mary Anne would take care of Andrew and Jason. Lionel, of course, could do whatever he wanted, which I was sure would include pestering us.

While everyone else was finishing up breakfast and clearing the table, Claud and I headed for the third floor of the west wing to make our beds and pack up some beach things. The moment we were away from the others, Claud and I started talking about the ghost.

"Let's check out the hallway for evidence," Claud said.

First we turned the hall light on and off a few times. No flickers. It worked perfectly. "The light we saw under the doorways looked like candlelight, anyway," Claud said. "It had a yellowy glow. The bulb in the hall light fixture gives off a pink glow."

I dropped to my hands and knees. "Let's

look for wax. Candles and dripping wax go together."

"I don't know if a ghost's candle would drip," Claud said.

"What's that?" I asked, pointing to a small, dark-orange blob on the carpet.

Claud knelt down and rubbed the spot with her finger. "Wax," she said. "And here's another spot."

And there were more. Not big hunks of wax, but fine little flecks of it here and there, all the way down the hall.

Suddenly a booming, sinister voice asked, "What are you do-o-ing?"

I was startled and afraid. Still, I looked up. Lionel was standing over us.

"Why are you crawling around on the floor?" he asked in his natural voice.

"Dawn dropped the back to an earring," Claud said.

I stood up. "Well, it's no big deal. Let's go to the beach."

"If it's not a big deal why did you look in the first place?" Lionel asked as he swung around and entered his room.

Claud and I exchanged a look. "What is it with him?" I asked in a whisper.

"Maybe he knows something about the wax

on the rug," Claud said. "Maybe he's our ghost."

I nodded. Lionel was a strong suspect.

During the next half an hour we made beds and helped the kids pack up for the beach. Then we headed down the long drive toward the gate. We must have been a sight — ten kids of all ages loaded with picnic baskets, beach toys, towels, etc. Maybe that's why the dark, handsome guy we saw walking toward us was smiling. Or was he laughing? It was hard to tell, because he was wearing reflective sunglasses.

Here's what the stranger looked like — one of those brooding teenage rebel loners. A sinister one, with his black T-shirt, black jeans, and those sunglasses. But it wasn't the clothes that made him seem sinister as much as his looks. He had straight black hair, heavy eyebrows, and a crooked smile.

"Hi," he said when he reached us.

"Hi," we all answered.

He'd stopped, so we did too.

"Can we help you?" efficient Kristy asked.

"I work here," he said. Just as I was thinking I wished he'd take off his sunglasses so I could see his eyes, he did. They were dark brown and alight with interest. Or was that an evil glint? The guy was really hard to read.

"You must be the Menders kids," he said. "I didn't know there were so many of you. Good thing the house is big."

There was that crooked smile again. Was it sinister or friendly? He was making me nervous.

"I'm Georgio Trono," he said as he extended a hand to shake with Claudia.

"I'm Claudia Kishi," she replied. "And we don't all live here. Some of us are baby-sitting for the — " Claud gestured around at the younger kids " — others." I could tell she was flustered, especially when Georgio's handshake lasted a few seconds longer than a handshake should. Georgio, whether he was friendly or not, was definitely a flirt. And he was flirting with Claud.

Kristy took care of the rest of the introductions. Then Georgio told us that his grandparents had been the caretakers of the mansion when Mr. Randolph was alive. "They're retired now," he explained, "but I'm still the summer gardener here. I practically lived here when I was a kid. What rooms are you guys staying in?"

We told him the west wing of the third floor and I mentioned that the house was so big we hadn't even been on the fourth floor yet.

Georgio's smile disappeared. "Don't go up there!" he said in a firm voice.

"Why not?" Claud asked.

"For one thing, the widow's walk isn't safe," he said. "And there're bats and . . ." He paused before adding, ". . . who knows what else in the attic."

I felt a chill run down my spine. No one said anything for a second.

Georgio smiled again. "But don't let that ruin your vacation. Reese is a great place."

We let out a collective sigh of relief and said good-bye. Georgio kept going toward the mansion, and we headed toward the gate.

"Wow," Mary Anne whispered to me. "Did you see the way he looked at Claud?"

We ran to Claud who was walking between Karen and Martha. "Karen and Martha, why don't you race to the gate?" I suggested. "We'll carry your stuff."

As soon as Karen and Martha were "on your mark, get set, gone," Mary Anne and I both asked Claud what she had thought about the mysterious Georgio.

"He's a Babe," Claud said. "But I have an uneasy feeling about him. I wonder why he doesn't want us to go to the fourth floor?"

"And why is he so interested in what rooms

we're staying in?" Mary Anne asked.

"He gives me the creeps," I said. "I can't explain it, but I don't trust him."

"Me, either," Claud said. But I noticed that she was looking dreamy, and was gently rubbing the palm of the hand Georgio had shaken.

When we arrived at the beach we put Georgio out of our minds and concentrated on getting our blankets laid out and the kids coated with sunblock. Just being on a beach, any beach, reminds me of California and makes me feel homesick for my life there. That's been happening to me more and more lately — missing California, I mean.

Lionel put on his sunglasses and checked out the beach for any "actor-types." In ten minutes he gave us his evaluation. "Only conservative, family types. No one sophisticated. No one hip. No one cool. Reese is one big fat no-place. I'll see you all back at the mansion." Oh, no. Were we losing Lionel so quickly? We were supposed to be helping him adjust.

"Come on, Lionel," I said. "Hang out here. It's a little early for the hip crowd. In California, nobody who's anybody shows up at the beach before noon. Have a little patience."

"How do you know what they do in California?" he asked.

Dawn

Mary Anne and Kristy answered in unison, "She's *from* California!"

Lionel's face lit up. "You are?"

When I told him I'd grown up in California and lived there most of my life, he sat down next to me.

Lionel asked me dozens of questions about California and the Hollywood movie scene. Fortunately, I had had a lot of actor sightings. And, since the father of one of my best California friends is a movie producer, I'd even met a few famous actors. Lionel was thrilled.

"Boy," Lionel said, "why couldn't Uncle Edward have had a mansion in L.A.? I'd have moved there in an instant!"

While we were talking, Mary Anne was building a castle with Karen and Martha, and Andrew was burying Kristy's feet and legs in sand. I saw Karen introduce herself to two girls who she then brought over to work on the sand castle. But Martha, meanwhile, stood up and walked to the edge of the water. She was pretending, as far as I could tell, that she didn't know Karen. Mary Anne signaled me to take over at the sand castle while she talked to Martha. I excused myself from Lionel's company and approached Karen and her new "friends."

I could hear Karen telling the other girls,

"You will love Martha. She is so much fun."
Then Karen called out, "Come on, Martha,
build with us. Everyone wants to meet you."

Poor shy Martha, I thought. This is not what
she needs. While Mary Anne took Martha's
hand and walked down the beach with her, I
squatted next to Karen. (In a flash, Jill was
right there beside me.) "Can we help?" I asked
Karen.

"Sure," she answered.

"Great," I said. I played with them for
awhile, but the sea was beckoning. "I'll be
right back," I said.

Jill, who an instant before had seemed extremely enthusiastic about sand castle building, stood up, too. "Where are you going?"
she asked as she brushed the sand off her
knees. "I want to do whatever the *teenagers*
do." I'd been thinking that if Jill were working
on the sand castle it would be easier for Martha
to join in later. Scratch that. Jill was going for
a swim with me. Which meant I couldn't go
out as far as I wanted. Or even have two minutes to myself to think about the haunted
house and the orange wax, or to wonder about
Georgio.

Jason, meanwhile, was sitting alone on his
towel. He'd moved himself farther down the
beach, so as not to look as if he were at the

beach with seven girls. I waved to him. "Come on, Jason. We're going for a swim."

He shook his head glumly and lay down. Lionel, who was now reading a book of plays, ignored his little brother. He didn't even seem to notice — or care — that Jason was isolating himself from the rest of us.

Once again I realized that while the Menders kids were all perfectly nice, sitting for them was not going to be easy.

After a swim in the ocean, more sand castle building, and a terrific picnic lunch courtesy of the Coopers, Claud suggested we pack up our stuff and go for a walk through town.

By then Lionel had given up on finding the in-crowd at Reese beach and headed back to the mansion. The rest of us made for the strip of shops and restaurants that lined the streets near the harbor. Kristy spotted a sporting goods store and steered Jason in that direction. "We'll catch up with you later," she told the rest of us.

We headed into a T-shirt shop that sold just the kinds of souvenirs we wanted. I noticed a big community bulletin board. "Let's check it out," I suggested. "We might find some ideas for things we can do with the kids."

"There's an announcement about the historical society," Mary Anne said. "Right here in town."

Claud said, "And look at this." She pointed to a big blue and white poster. "Reese is celebrating its two hundred and fiftieth birthday. Founders' Day. There's going to be a parade with floats."

"And a carnival and rides and everything," Karen said. "Goody."

"It's next Saturday," I added. "We'll still be here."

By then Kristy and Jason had joined us. Kristy was beaming, which meant that the trip to the sporting goods store had been good for Jason. "I got a new softball," he told us.

We showed Kristy the poster for Founders' Day. "Uh-oh," Kristy said. I had a feeling she was remembering a few other times that Claud had persuaded us to dress up for parades. The members of the BSC have gone to some outrageous extremes to provide Claud with opportunities to express her artistic talent.

Claud told the younger kids how much fun it would be to dress up and be in a parade together.

Karen jumped up and down and shouted, "Yea! We are going to ride on a float. Everybody will see us."

Dawn

Martha just stood there shaking her head no. "Maybe Martha could help me with the research, and make the costumes," Mary Anne said. Then she whispered to Martha, just loudly enough for us to hear, "I don't like to be in parades either."

"I'll be in it if Dawn is," Jill said. (So what else was new?)

"Maybe we could make a historical float," Mary Anne mused, "since we're in historical New England and it is an historical celebration."

Jason was reading every last announcement on the bulletin board. "What's summer stock?" he asked. "Is that like stock cars? I'd go to the stock car races, I mean if there were some guys to go with."

We gathered around him to read the poster that had caught his attention. "Summer stock is theatrical productions put on during the summer," I explained. "You know, plays."

"You find summer stock in tourist areas, like historic New England," Mary Anne added.

"Oh," said Jason. He sounded disappointed.

"The play that's on while we're here is *Dracula*," Kristy said.

"Just what we need," Claud said with a shiver. "Something scary."

"But maybe it's just what Lionel needs," I said. I was getting an idea. "Lionel thinks there aren't any actors around here," I continued. "But this actor, the one who plays Count Dracula, is famous. Not like a leading, leading man. But his name's always in the newspapers in L.A., for one thing or another. I bet Lionel will recognize it."

Mary Anne wrote down the actor's name, the dates and times of the performances, and the price of the tickets. She'd also taken careful notes on the days and times the historical society was open, and on the particulars for Founders' Day. That's our Mary Anne — BSC secretary.

As we headed back to the mansion with our troop of kids, I felt pretty good about our first day in Reese. It was the nighttime I was worried about. And, as it turned out, I had good reason to worry about it.

CHAPTER 5

Jessi

Today's special meeting of the BSC went great. We notified clients about our reassigned jobs, and took on some new ones besides. I hope the Reese division of the BSC is having a fun vacation knowing that the club is in good hands.

"Let's take turns being acting president," Mal said. "You go first, and I'll be secretary."

It was one o'clock on Sunday and Mal and I were conducting a special meeting of the BSC. The meeting was held in Claudia's room, of course. I loved it. I, Jessi Ramsey, age eleven, was acting president of the Baby-sitters Club. I sat in Kristy's director's chair and put on her visor. Mal lay across Claud's bed with the record book in front of her. So far there were only two people attending the meeting — us.

We knew that Logan wouldn't be there, because he was working the Sunday brunch shift at the Rosebud Cafe. But he had given Mal his work schedule for the next ten days so we'd know when he was free to baby-sit. "Just call and let me know when you need me," he said. He's a really nice guy. No wonder Mary Anne likes him so much.

The other person who was supposed to be attending the meeting was Shannon, of course. But she hadn't arrived yet.

When she finally walked in at 1:14 I said, "This meeting of the Baby-sitters Club — "

"Hey, guys," Shannon said, "don't you even say hi?"

Mal and I both said hi to her. Shannon sat

59

on Claud's desk and said, "My dad's picking me up here at one-thirty so we better get started."

Mal and I exchanged a glance. Who was running this meeting anyway? Shannon would *never* act that way if Kristy were sitting in the director's chair.

I sat tall and said, "This is a special meeting of the Baby-sitters Club. The first order of business is to call clients to tell them they're getting a different sitter from the one they were originally assigned." I turned to secretary Mallory and asked, "Who do we call first?"

"The Kuhns," she answered. "They're expecting Kristy tomorrow at ten. You're taking her place."

Jake Kuhn answered the phone. I told him that Kristy had an out-of-town job and I would be sitting for him, Laurel, and Patsy the next day.

"That's awful," he moaned.

"What?" I asked. "What's awful?"

"I want Kristy to sit. She said she'd practice softball with me."

"I know how to play softball," I told him.

"But Kristy's my coach. She was going to teach me how to throw a knuckleball. Do you know how to throw a knuckleball?"

I had to tell him that I didn't. I'd have to

think of something extra-special to do with Jake.

My next phone call was to the Kormans. Melody wasn't any happier than Jake was about having a substitute sitter. "I was going to ask Mary Anne to teach me how to make doll clothes," she complained.

"Mallory can help you make up stories about your dolls," I suggested.

"But my dolls don't have any clothes!" Melody whined.

I made sure to tell Mal that Melody wanted to make doll clothes. Knowing Mal, she'd come up with some nifty ideas for dressing dolls before she baby-sat for Melody.

I made three more calls to clients explaining substitutions. Fortunately those calls went a little better than my first two.

When I'd finished the last call Shannon asked, "Did you listen to the messages on the answering machine?"

"That's what we're doing next," I said. I didn't tell her that I'd forgotten about the answering machine. It's a good thing Shannon thought of it, because the Prezziosos, the Arnolds, and the Hobarts had all called needing sitters.

I called Mrs. Prezzioso first. She said she needed two sitters for Monday afternoon. "My sister-in-law and her twins are visiting," she explained. "They're two-year-old boys and of course there's Jenny and the baby."

"Okay," I said, "we'll call you right back."

We checked our schedules. I was sitting for the Kuhns all day. Logan was working at the Rosebud Cafe. Shannon was sitting at my house for Becca and Squirt.

"I can handle the job alone," Mal said, "if Mrs. Prezzioso doesn't mind. I take care of my brothers. Twins will be a piece of cake after triplets."

I called Mrs. Prezzioso back and she agreed. "Just warn Mallory," Mrs. Prezzioso said, "that my nephews are a handful."

The next call was to Mrs. Hobart. She needed a sitter for Wednesday night. Logan was working at the Rosebud, but Shannon was free and she said she'd take the job.

A horn honked outside the Kishis' house. "Uh-oh," Shannon said. "It's one-thirty. And there's my ride. Gotta go." As she was leaving she added, "Next time let's try to end on time." She walked out of the room.

"How about *starting* on time?" I mumbled.

Shannon poked her head back in the room. Had she heard me? "You guys," she said, "don't be discouraged. You're doing a great job. Sorry I was late today."

"That's okay," I said. "See you Monday at — "

" — five-thirty," we said in unison.

"But I can't make it," Shannon said. "That's what I came back to tell you. I'll leave you a message on the machine about when I can sit."

After Shannon left we called the Arnolds. They needed a sitter Monday night at seven-thirty for Carolyn and Marilyn. "I'll call you right back," I told Mrs. Arnold.

"Shannon's already sitting," Mal said. "And neither of us can do it because it's at night. But Monday Logan gets off work from the Rosebud at six-thirty, so he can probably start a sitting job at seven-thirty. Tell Mrs. Arnold that Logan will sit."

"Shouldn't we call Logan first?" I asked.

"He said not to call him at work," Mal reminded me. "I'll call and tell him later."

I phoned Mrs. Arnold again and told her Logan would be there at seven-thirty on Monday night.

"Thank goodness," she said. "Mr. Arnold and I are hosting the auction for Stoneybrook Ambulance Services. I don't know what I would have done if I couldn't find a sitter."

"I'm glad we can help, Mrs. Arnold," I said.

I felt pretty good when I hung up the phone. The BSC was an important part of the community. And Mal and I were running it.

"This meeting of the Baby-sitters Club is adjourned," I told Mallory in a deep-voiced, serious tone.

She broke into giggles. I did too. As we were leaving Claudia's room Mal said, "That was a great meeting, pres."

I looked at my watch. "Uh-oh," I said, "I better get a move on. I have a job at the Mancusis' in ten minutes."

As I ran down the street I wondered how things were going for the Reese division of the BSC.

CHAPTER 6

Kristy

Sunday night
10:00 p.m.

Tonight I caught the "ghost" in the act. Unfortunately, it seems he's not the only one. Ghost, I mean. Guys, we have to be extra careful not to let on to the rest of the Menders kids that there are some very weird things going on in their new home. They're having enough trouble getting into the swing of things in Reese.

Sunday night was a perfect night for a bar-becue. Elton Cooper grilled burgers, hot dogs, and chicken for us. After spending most of the day outside, at the beach and in town, we had big appetites. Elton is not as friendly as his wife, which is strange since he can talk and she can't. But boy does he know his barbecue.

After supper we were sitting around the ver-anda table, talking about Founders' Day.

"I think making a float is a great idea," Mrs. Menders said.

Martha ran to her mother and whispered something in her ear. "But, of course, not everyone has to be *on* the float," Mrs. Menders added.

"Martha and I are behind-the-scenes help-ers," Mary Anne told the Menderses.

I could see that Karen was about to make a case for Martha's being on the float, so I said, "Karen, would you please go up to my room to find Andrew's *Frog and Toad* book?"

"If Martha will come with me," Karen said.

As the girls were leaving the porch I heard Karen tell Martha, "We could have a float about animals. You would make a perfect cat. Everyone loves cats. It would make you very popular."

"Dress-up is for girls," Jason told whoever

would listen. "I'm not going to be on any dumb float."

"Count me out," Lionel told Claudia. "It's too makeshift and unprofessional for me."

Claud always has trouble getting us psyched up for her parade floats. But the Menders kids were really going to be a challenge.

The adults announced that they wanted to go into town to see how busy the stores were in the evening, so I said we'd be happy to take care of the kids.

After they left, Dawn (and Jill) started a conversation with Lionel about the summer stock theater while Claud and Mary Anne cleared the table. "Come on, Jason," Claud said. "Let's have a little help here."

"Oh, okay," Jason said. "I'll carry the heavy stuff for you."

When Karen and Martha returned, I moved to the edge of the veranda, where the porch light would fall on the pages of the book. Andrew climbed on my lap. Martha and Karen sat on either side of me. *Frog and Toad Together,*" I read from the cover, "by Arnold Lobel." I looked around at the kids. "This book has a whole bunch of little stories. Should I read them in the order they're in the book?"

"Yes," Martha said.

"Read them all," said Karen.

"Rib-bid," added Andrew.

By the time I came to the last story in the book, Karen was reading all Toad's lines and Lionel — who was now standing behind me — was reading Frog's lines. (I hate to admit it, but he was good.) I did the narration. The others had finished carrying things back to the kitchen and were listening to us.

When I said "the end," Andrew looked up at me and said, "Kristy, I want to be a frog *and* a toad in the parade."

Karen said that Andrew couldn't be both a frog and a toad. That they were two different kinds of animals.

"Well they're sort of alike," Jill said. "They both hop and live in ponds."

"Do they?" Andrew asked me.

"Toads live in the grass and under rocks," I said. "Frogs live in ponds. But I don't know much more than that."

Dawn went inside to find a dictionary. When she returned with one we looked up "frog" and "toad" and read the definitions out loud. Mary Anne pointed out that a frog's skin is smooth and moist while a toad's is rough and dry.

Andrew looked more curious than ever. "You know what, Andrew?" I said. "Let's go *find* some frogs and toads and you can *see* the difference."

Elton Cooper, who was putting the cover on the grill, overheard us. "You'll find frogs in that little pond behind the old gardener's cottage," he said. "Go down the path that starts near the kitchen door and follow it through the pine grove. The cottage is back there. I'll bring you a flashlight."

Lionel decided to skip our "little excursion," as he called it. Jason said he was going to his room to organize his baseball cards. With Lionel promising to keep an eye on his younger brother, the rest of us were free to go on our frog and toad hunt.

I was glad Elton thought of the flashlight because it was a moonless, dark night. Once we were away from the house we wouldn't have been able to see each other, much less toads and frogs.

We found a toad under a rock at the edge of the rose garden. "This toad is small," Andrew said.

"It's so cute," Karen added. She did a terrific imitation of a toad's jump for Andrew.

I led everybody along the path Mr. Cooper had described. It was pitch-black in the pine grove. When I turned to look back at the house, I thought that it looked . . . different.

Mary Anne thought so, too. Her voice was trembling when she whispered in my ear, "Look. There's a light on. On the *top floor*. The one with the attic and the old servants' quarters. I thought nobody went up there." We stood still, staring at the mansion while Claud and Dawn continued walking with the kids.

Suddenly, the light went off and the top floor was dark again. What was going on? Who was up there?

"Come on, slow pokes," Claud called back to us.

Mary Anne and I caught up with the others in front of the gardener's cottage. "Isn't it neat?" Claud said. She sounded cheerful, so I knew she hadn't seen the light. To me the cottage looked a little rundown and spooky.

"It would be fun to play in there," Karen said. "Can Martha and I use it for our playhouse?"

"It's too far from the main house," I told her. "Besides, you have plenty of other things to do." I took Andrew by one hand and Karen by the other. With all this weird stuff going on, I wanted to keep the kids as close to me as possible.

The excursion was giving me the creeps. If it hadn't been for Andrew pulling on my hand

and saying, "I want to see a frog," I would have turned back then.

We found the pond and, after a bit of searching, we found a frog, too. Then another. Andrew spoke in rib-bid language to both of them.

"Okay, guys," I said, "we've seen one toad and two frogs. Let's head back. It's late."

Dawn, Jill, and Claud took the lead on the path. Mary Anne and I followed with Karen, Martha, and Andrew. I glanced up at the house. A chill ran down my spine. The top floor window was lit up again. Claud ran back to me. "Did you see that?" she whispered. She was pretty spooked, too. Especially since by the time we reached the back door, we'd seen it go out again.

It was a relief to return to the big kitchen and Margaret Cooper's pleasant smile. Even gruff Elton's presence made me feel less frightened.

"Find any frogs?" he asked.

"Rib-bid, Rib-bid," Andrew answered.

We all laughed. Even Margaret. I guess with some vocal cord problems you can still laugh.

"Yes, we did," I said as I handed Elton the flashlight. "Thanks for this."

"Let's go, kids," Dawn said. "I'll take you upstairs. It's bedtime."

"And storytime," Karen added.

"I'll come, too," Mary Anne said.

"What can we do to help you in here, Mr. Cooper?" Claud asked.

"You could count out the morning dishes and silverware," he said. "And please, call me Elton. And my wife's name is Margaret."

I thought again how nice the Coopers — Elton and Margaret — were, and what a long workday they'd had, with all the cooking and cleaning. I was glad to help them. And maybe they could help me, too . . . with the mystery.

While I was counting out spoons I casually asked Elton, "Does anybody ever go up to the top floor?"

"Oh, no," he said. "It hasn't been used in years, maybe decades. I've never been up there myself."

"That's strange," Claud said. "When we were out just now we saw a light go on in one of the rooms in the west wing of the fourth floor."

"Off and on," I said. "First it was on. Then it was off. Then it went on again. And off."

"Couldn't be," Elton said. "The door to the stairway leading up there is locked. I've heard tell there were strange goings-on up there some years ago. That's probably when it was closed off."

"What kind of goings-on?" Claud asked.

Margaret Cooper rapped the kitchen counter with a wooden spoon and shook her head no. I had a feeling she didn't want her husband to tell us what they knew about the top floor.

"It's nothing for your young ears to hear," he said. "Besides, that was then and this is now."

Margaret put her right arm out straight in front of herself and moved it in a circle.

"My wife thinks maybe it was the lighthouse light reflecting off the windows that you saw," Elton explained.

"Yeah," I said. "Maybe."

After we put our charges to sleep, the Reese contingent of the BSC met in Mary Anne's room. Andrew was already asleep in mine. My friends and I were seriously frightened.

Claud went to the window and looked out over the sea. "There's no way the beam from the lighthouse could have reflected on that window," she told us. "We were looking at the back of the house. It's the *front* of the house that faces the ocean and the lighthouse."

"Maybe Lionel did it," Mary Anne said. "He was inside. Maybe he was checking out the fourth floor. It is his house."

It sounded as if Mary Anne was hoping with

all her heart that Lionel was responsible for the light on the top floor. But I had to remind her, "Elton said the door to the staircase is locked and no one has a key."

"I know you guys don't want to admit this," Dawn said, "but the house *could* be haunted by ghosts. A ghost in the hall last night. And one on the fourth floor tonight."

"Please, Dawn, don't say that," Mary Anne said. "There has to be an explanation."

"We did see that wax on the rug," Claud said.

"Who says a ghost can't use real candles?" Dawn asked.

Nobody had an answer for that. And since we weren't making any progress, we decided to head for our rooms. Dawn, Claudia, and I had already stood up. Then we heard it again. *"Ohh-hh. Ohh-hh."* This time it was a high-pitched and eerie voice. I leaned over and turned off Mary Anne's bedside lamp. We all stared at the slit under the door. Candlelight flickered there. My heart pounded. Maybe Dawn was right, and this house was haunted.

Then I had a hunch. There was no time to discuss it with the others. I drew in a deep breath, and tiptoed to the door. I almost turned back when I heard that *"ohh-hh, ohh-hh,"* again. But even though my heart was pounding practically out of my chest by then, I reached over, grabbed the knob and threw the door open.

My terrified friends gasped. I screeched. But a minute later, we were laughing. Because in the doorway stood a very startled "ghost" — Lionel.

"Oops," he said. "You weren't supposed to do that. It wasn't in the script."

We were so relieved to have solved the mystery of the hallway ghost that we couldn't stop laughing. Even Lionel loosened up and laughed with us. By then we were standing in the hall.

"Very, very funny," Dawn said. "And the lights on the fourth floor tonight, Lionel. That was really good. You deserve the special effects Academy Award."

"What lights on the fourth floor?" Lionel asked.

"Lionel, we know you were up there turning the lights on and off," I said.

"I wouldn't go up there alone," he protested. "I'd be too afraid. Besides, the door's locked."

I didn't believe him. After all, he was an actor. Dawn didn't believe him either. "Lionel," she said, "if you don't confess right now, I'll never, ever tell you another thing about Hollywood, not even the tiniest bit of gossip."

"That's not fair," Lionel said. "You guys — gals — are all crazy."

Just then I heard footsteps. Coming from upstairs. The others must have heard them, too, because everybody was looking up. And I had a feeling they were all thinking what I was thinking — upstairs is the fourth floor. The floor nobody can reach because the door is locked.

As good an actor as Lionel was, he couldn't have pretended the fear that drained the color from his face. Claud, Mary Anne, and I huddled close to one another. They looked as pale as Lionel. I was feeling a little faint and weak in the knees myself.

"Wha-at's tha-at?" Mary Anne managed to stutter.

I put my fears aside. "That's just Spooky thumping around," I said. I pretended a loud yawn and talked loudly and cheerfully to cover up any more sounds from above. "So," I said, "it's time to get to our rooms. It was fun fooling around with you about all this ghost stuff, Lionel." I gave him a little push in the direction of his room. "Let's go, everyone. Nighty-night."

I shot Claud a meaningful glance that said, Help me here. Good old Claud caught right on. "We had you really going there, didn't we, Lionel?" she said, attempting a laugh.

Lionel looked a little confused. "Yeah," he said. "You win. I'll never play a trick on you again." He walked off toward his room, mumbling something about "hysterical females."

As soon as he was gone we heard the footsteps again. We ran into Mary Anne's room and closed the door.

"You guys," I said, "no matter how frightened we are, we have to protect the kids, even Lionel, from what's going on in the mansion."

"But Kristy," Dawn protested, "maybe he's the one who's doing all this stuff. He did try to scare us by pretending to be a ghost."

"But how could he make those noises upstairs?" Claud asked. "He was *with* us."

"Maybe he has an accomplice," Dawn said.

We talked about that for awhile. But in the end we agreed that Lionel probably wasn't responsible for the lights on the fourth floor. Then, I wondered, who — or what — was?

"Mary Anne," I said, "do you want to sleep in my room tonight?"

"Yes," she said in a quavering voice. "Yes I do." Dawn and Claud said they were going to double up, too.

Mary Anne fell asleep with a pillow over her head. Andrew was sound asleep in his

Kristy

little bed. But I lay wide-awake for hours, waiting for more ghostly sounds and thinking about all the scary things that had happened since we'd arrived at the Randolph mansion. I don't know what was more frightening, remembering what had already happened, or worrying about what would happen next.

CHAPTER 7

Claudia

Monday
6:00 p.m.

I cant beleve all thats gone on since we came here Saterday night. Thanks for wrighting it all down evrybody. This notebok will be a big help when I rite my compositon for mrs. Hall. By the way, I'm not worried about having somthing intresting to write about!

"Come on, Claud. Wake up. We need to do some major detective work today, and this might be the only chance we have to talk privately."

Dawn was leaning over me from the side of her bed. I looked up at her from the nest of blankets I'd made for myself on the floor. "Ghosts," I said sleepily. "I dreamed about ghosts."

"That wasn't a dream," Dawn said. "We heard one again last night. Remember?"

It all came back in a rush. The footsteps above our heads. The blood-curdling scream in the night. Dawn was right. We did have some major detective work to do. I just hoped I was brave enough to do it.

By the time Jill came knocking on our door to find out what Dawn was going to wear, we had a plan for the day that included sleuthing.

"I'm going to wear a sundress and sandals," Dawn told Jill. Then she added, "Claud and I thought you girls might like to go to the library today. We'll help you sign up for cards and check out some books."

"And I'm going to do some research while we're there," I added, "for a composition I have to write."

Now Karen and Martha were in Dawn's

bedroom, too. "What are you going to do research on?" Karen asked.

"I'm going to see if I can find out about the history of the Randolph estate," I said. "So let's all get dressed, eat breakfast, and head to town."

I decided to wear my floral-print mini-sundress (the pink and red flower pattern is big and sort of abstract). To that I added a pink baseball cap, dangling yellow glass earrings, and my red high-top sneakers.

After breakfast Dawn and I were ready to take the girls to the library. As we walked around the side of the mansion toward the driveway Karen grabbed my hand and tugged on it. "Claudia," she said. "That guy is here again."

I looked around and, sure enough, there was Georgio running across the lawn toward us. There was no way to avoid him.

"Hi," he said when he reached us. "How's it going?"

"Okay," Dawn answered.

Just as he had done the day before, Georgio checked out my clothes. When you dress the way I do you have to expect people to notice. But when Georgio looked at me I felt uncomfortable. Did he think I was *too* wild and colorful?

"We are going to the library," Karen told him. "To check out some books for us. And Claudia is going to — "

" — choose some books, too," I said, completing Karen's sentence. Suddenly, I didn't want Karen to tell Georgio that I was going to research the Randolph mansion. I was suspicious of him, and when you're suspicious of someone, you're careful about what you tell him. (I learned that from all the Nancy Drew mysteries I've read.) To keep the conversation off me, I asked Georgio, "How's it going?"

"Great," Georgio said. "Except I need some advice. I was hoping you could help me."

I didn't even know the guy and he wanted my advice!? Advice about what? School? Family problems? Girls? How to menace a houseful of kids?

"Advice about what?" Dawn asked.

"I've noticed that Claudia has terrific taste in clothes," he said. "And puts colors together in a great way." He was looking me right in the eye. "I'm putting in some new rosebushes and I can't decide which colors to plant where. I wondered if you could help me, Claudia."

"Yeah, sure," I replied. "I guess."

"I'll go ahead with the kids," Dawn said. "We'll meet you at the library." She flashed me one of those we'll-leave-you-two-alone grins.

When they'd gone, Georgio told me, "The rose garden's on the other side of the house."

Part of me wanted to call out to Dawn, "Wait up. I'm coming with you guys." But another part of me was happy to follow Georgio. Well, I thought, this is a day devoted to detection and since Georgio is sort of a suspect, I'd better follow him. Besides, I can never resist an artistic challenge.

Twenty-five rosebushes were waiting to be planted. Five each of five shades of red and pink. Georgio told me that Mr. Randolph had ordered them from a nursery before he died. "He loved roses," Georgio said. "This will be like a memorial garden for him."

"That's really nice," I replied. I studied the rosebushes for a few minutes, then I asked, "Can we take one rose petal from each bush?"

"Whatever helps," he answered.

When we'd collected the twenty-five rose petals, I sat on a stone bench in the middle of the garden and moved the petals around until I was happy with the arrangement. While I worked with the colors, Georgio turned over soil.

After about ten minutes I called to him. We

looked at the rows of petals I'd arranged on the bench. "This is the layout I would use," I said. "What do you think?"

"I think it's perfect," he replied. "But could you wait until I have the bushes placed around the garden before you go? That way I'll be sure to follow your plan exactly."

I walked around the paths of the garden and helped him place the bushes where he'd later plant them. "How are you going to find an outlet for your artistic talent around here?" he asked.

"I'm always doing art projects with the kids I sit for," I told him. I was thinking of the float we were planning for the Founders' Day parade, but decided not to mention it to Georgio.

"You should make a float with the kids for the Founders' Day parade," he said. Could he read my mind?

"Maybe I will," I told him. "Being in a town parade would be a nice way to end our vacation here."

"I thought you were going to be here all summer," he said. He sounded disappointed. But then he added, with that hard to read grin of his, "Well, Claudia, let's make the most of the time you have."

What did he mean by that?

"I could help you make that float," he said. "I can build props and you can use my pickup truck."

His pickup truck? I wondered how old you had to be to get a driver's license in Maine. Was he sixteen plus or eighteen plus? I didn't tell Georgio that if we borrowed his pickup truck for the float we'd have to borrow him to drive it, too.

"Um, I better get going," I said. "Babysitting, you know."

"First let me show you a picture of the float some friends and I made last year," he said. "It's in the shed. Come on. It'll only take a minute."

"All the way to the pond?" I said. "It'll take a lot more than a minute."

"You're thinking of the gardener's cottage," he said. "Where my grandparents used to live. The shed's just around by the garage. That's where I keep my tools."

As we walked to the shed, Georgio told me he used to stay in the gardener's cottage by the pond with his grandparents during the summer. "Since no one else is using it," he said, "I still sleep there sometimes."

The shed was small and dark. All my fears about Georgio came flooding back. I wished I hadn't followed him there. I bumped into a big lumpy something and let out a shriek of terror. Was it a dead body?

"What happened?" Georgio asked.

In the half light I made out that the "corpse" was a big bag of sand or something.

"I just bumped into this — stuff," I told Georgio.

"I don't want anything to happen to you," he said. I couldn't tell if he was smiling at me or smirking when he said that. Finally he pulled a cord that switched on an overhead lightbulb. We were facing a wall of neatly arranged tools. There were saws, knives, hammers, and weapon-like instruments. Georgio reached toward the ax. I was about to make a run for it when his hand landed on a photo that was pinned between the ax and a hammer. He took the photo down and showed it to me. I studied it. Georgio and six other kids were posed in the back of his pickup truck. Their theme was the sixties, so they were dressed like hippies. The pickup truck was painted in psychedelic colors.

"Does your truck still look like that?" I asked.

He laughed. "We used washable paint. Otherwise, I would have been the laughingstock on campus this year."

I practically choked on the next question. "Are you in college?"

"University of Maine," he said. "Some of these guys on the float were a year ahead of me in high school. And a couple were in tenth grade. I don't make a big deal about age. Some of my friends are a couple of years older than me. Some are a couple of years younger. Like you. You're sixteen, am I right?"

I just nodded. Why didn't I tell him right then that I was thirteen? Maybe I was afraid he'd be mad at me for not having told him sooner. Or maybe I was just keeping to the detective's rule: Don't give information to the suspect without a good reason. Or maybe I thought he'd think twice about talking to me so much if he knew how young I was. And the truth was that I wasn't so spooked by him anymore. I was kind of enjoying becoming friends with Georgio Trono.

"Anyway," he said. "That was our float."

"It's great," I said. Something else in the shed caught my eye. A candle. An orange candle. A wave of fear coursed through my body. I stepped back from Georgio. Suddenly I wasn't feeling so good about being with him.

"I really have to go," I said. " 'Bye."

I burst through the doorway and into the daylight. Then I ran all the way down the long driveway. Lionel had been our "ghost" last night, I knew. Had Georgio been the "ghost" in the hallway the night before that? Just how involved was he?

When I reached the Reese public library my heart was still pounding. I found Dawn in the children's room. She was simultaneously helping Jill pick out a book and attempting to stop Karen from introducing Martha to every kid there. This wasn't the time for me to report to Dawn about the incriminating evidence I had found in the gardener's shed.

I edged Karen away from a bunch of five-year-olds and their day camp counselor. Somehow I convinced her that we should go to the pillow corner for some quiet reading time. As we passed Dawn and Jill, Dawn handed me a book. "It's a history of Reese," she said. "The librarian found it for us."

I took the book to the pillow corner and plopped down with Karen and Martha. "*A Historical Tour of Reese,*" the title read, "by Millicent Ellsworth." I turned to the index in the back of the book and found two references to the Randolph mansion: Randolph, Mary Sears, p. 108, and Randolph, Reginald, p. 69.

On page 69 I read that Reginald Randolph had been a wealthy landholder and fisherman. He had owned a big fleet of fishing boats, and dozens of fishermen had worked for him. He often captained one of the boats himself. On one of those fishing trips, in 1859, Reginald Randolph and a crew of thirteen had been lost at sea.

Turning to page 108 I learned that Reginald's wife, Mary, mourned her husband for the remaining twenty years of her life. From ten o'clock until eleven o'clock every night, Mary, dressed in white, stood on the widow's walk of the mansion and stared out at the sea. The townspeople of that time reported seeing her standing there even in the foulest weather. During a fierce storm in 1879, she was hurled to her death by the winds.

I wrote down names and dates in my notebook. Mary Sears Randolph was an obvious candidate for our fourth-floor ghost. I couldn't wait to tell the others.

When we returned to the mansion everyone was gathering on the veranda for lunch. The Coopers carried out platters of sandwiches, salad, cookies, and fruit. Lisa suggested that the BSC members might enjoy a break from the kids during lunch. "Thanks," Kristy said.

"That's a great idea," I added.

So the Reese contingent of the BSC took our lunches to a picnic table under a big oak tree. (I was relieved to see that Mrs. Menders was making certain that Jill didn't trail after us.)

Before I could tell everybody what I'd learned about Mary Sears Randolph, Mary Anne said, "Claud, I saw you talking to Georgio again. What was that all about?"

I told my friends about helping lay out the rosebushes, and how Georgio offered to help us with the float for the Founders' Day parade. I even told them about the neat sixties float he'd made with his friends.

"I think Georgio has a crush on you," Kristy put in.

"You guys," I said. "There's something I haven't told you yet. Actually, there're two things. One is that Georgio's *old* — he's in college and he has his driver's license."

"That means he could be nineteen, or even older," Dawn exclaimed. "Does he know how old you are, Claud?"

I shook my head no and went right on to the second thing I hadn't told them. "I saw an orange candle in the shed where he keeps his tools. A used one."

"Why would he have a candle in the toolshed?" Kristy asked.

"For light?" Mary Anne suggested. "Maybe there's no electricity in there."

"He turned on a light so I could see the

picture of his sixties float," I told them. "So the shed has electricity."

"Do you think he's the one who's been trying to scare us?" Dawn asked.

"But we know it was Lionel," Mary Anne said. "We caught him in the act."

"Lionel was carrying a white candle," Dawn pointed out. "The wax we found on the rug was dark orange."

"And we never asked Lionel if he was the one who scared us that first night," I said. "We just assumed he did."

"So, Claud, you're saying we could have two phony ghosts," Kristy said. "The Lionel ghost last night and the Georgio ghost the night before."

"What about the lights on the fourth floor?" Mary Anne asked.

"And the footsteps," Kristy added.

"And the scream we heard in the middle of the night," Dawn said.

"There's one more thing I haven't told you guys about Georgio," I said. "He sometimes sleeps in the gardener's cottage."

"You mean he might have been there last night, spying on us," Dawn said with a shudder. "That's creepy."

"Or maybe he wasn't in the cottage," Kristy

said, "but on the fourth floor of the mansion, turning lights off and on."

"But the door's locked," Mary Anne reminded us.

"He's been around the estate his whole life," I said. "He probably has a way of getting up there. Maybe there's a secret passage."

"So he could have been the one walking up and down in the fourth floor hall," Dawn said.

"And screaming in the middle of the night," I added.

"But why would Georgio want to scare us?" Mary Anne asked.

"That's the mystery," I said. "But there's one last thing you don't know." I finally told them the tragic story of Reginald Randolph who was lost at sea, and his wife's nightly vigil on the widow's walk.

We looked up at the widow's walk. I imagined Mary Randolph standing there in her white dress . . . every night . . . for twenty years. Even in the noon sun I shivered. I wondered if Mary was now spending her nights haunting the mansion? Or was someone else — Georgio, perhaps — trying to make us *think* the Randolph mansion was haunted?

CHAPTER 8

KAREN

MONDAY

DEAR DADDY,

HI FROM REESE, MAWE. THE HOUSE WE ARE STAYING IN IS A LOT BIGGER THAN THE BIG HOUSE. I AM HELPING THE BABY-SITTERS. MY JOB IS TO MAKE SURE MARTHA MENDERS MAKES FRIENDS IN HER NEW TOWN. IT IS A HARD JOB BECAUSE MARTHA IS SHY. BUT I WILL FIGURE IT OUT. I THINK IT IS LUCKY FOR HER THAT I AM NOT SHY.

YOUR DAUGHTER,
KAREN

P.S.
SEE YOU SOON.

P.P.S.
ANDREW SAYS HI-RIB-BID.

Reese is a small town. But there are lots of kids around. There were tons of them at the beach. And some at the library. I made a promise to myself. By the end of Monday, Martha Menders would have three new friends. And they would all be nice.

After lunch I helped Mary Anne straighten up the porch. "So what are we going to do this afternoon?" I asked her.

"There are some stores I'd like to check out in town," Mary Anne said. "It might be fun to start the afternoon there."

Goody. There would be lots of kids in the kinds of stores they have in Reese. They have one store called "Fudge Depot" that just sells fudge. And one next to it called "Mity Kites." You can guess what they sell. "I'll go get Martha," I told Mary Anne.

"I'm going to buy Claudia an early birthday present," Mary Anne said. "So don't invite her, okay?"

"Okay," I said.

I love secrets. And I am *great* at keeping secrets secret. I found Martha swinging in the hammock with Claudia. I told Martha that we were going to town with Mary Anne. Claudia said she might come, too. But I told her that Mary Anne had a *special reason* for not wanting her to go shopping with us. Claudia smiled and said, "I guess I'll just rest in the hammock instead of going with you."

"I'm going to stay here, too," Martha said. "I want to read *The Secret Garden*." That was the book she had checked out from the library.

I put on a pout and told Martha that I love shopping and I wanted to look for presents for my family. And that I needed her help. The pouting worked because Martha climbed out of the comfy hammock and came with me.

On the way to town Mary Anne asked Martha how she liked Reese so far. Martha said, "I want to go back to Boston. We live in a big apartment in a new building with an elevator. That's where my best friend Louise lives."

I thought I was Martha's best friend. At least while I was visiting her. Well, I would be her best friend soon. Just wait until I introduced her to a bunch of kids in Reese. I knew that Martha and I and all her new friends would have loads of fun together. I am like Kristy. I enjoy challenges.

"Here we are," Mary Anne said. "This is the store where I'm sure I'll find a good present for Claudia." It was an art supply store.

We went inside. Mary Anne and Martha walked up and down the aisles looking for the perfect present for Claudia. I walked up and down the aisles looking for the perfect friend for Martha. All I could find were teenagers or kids who were a lot younger than us. Boo, boo, boo.

My luck changed when Mary Anne was standing at the cash register buying a face painting set for Claudia. Martha was sticking to Mary Anne like glue. And I was looking at a pack of construction paper and thinking of what I could make with it.

Here is the good luck part. A girl my age (and Martha's) walked into the store with her mother. The girl looked familiar to me. Then I remembered why. I ran to her and said, "Hi. I saw you on the beach yesterday. You had on a red two-piece bathing suit with butterflies."

"Oh," was all the girl replied. Then she looked at the floor. Her mother said, "We were at the beach yesterday, but I don't remember that Amber played with you."

"We did not *officially* meet," I admitted. "But I noticed her. And I thought, that girl would like to meet my friend Martha. Martha Menders who just moved to Reese. Martha is loads of fun. So here she is — Martha Menders!" I turned to the cash register where Mary Anne and Martha had been standing. They were gone.

96

"I think your friends left," Amber's mother said.

I looked through the store window and saw that she was right. Martha and Mary Anne were already waiting outside for me. Martha was holding Mary Anne's hand and looking down at the sidewalk. But Mary Anne was looking at me. She signaled for me to come out.

I signaled for her to come back into the store. She shook her head no.

"I have to go now," I told Amber and her mother. "But do not forget," I added with a big smile. "Martha Menders. She is a great kid."

When I ran outside I told Mary Anne, "You should not have kept telling me to come out. You should have come back inside. I met a perfect friend for Martha. Her name is Amber and she is shy, too."

"Karen, I think you should let Martha meet people in her own way," Mary Anne said.

I did not think Mary Anne Spier was the best person to give me advice about how to help Martha meet people. After all, next to Martha, Mary Anne is the shyest person I know.

Now my stepsister, Kristy, is not shy. That is one of the things I love about her. And

Kristy knows how to take action and make things happen. So I was glad when we saw Kristy walking toward us on Main Street. (Jason and Andrew were with her.)

"Where are you guys going?" I asked.

Kristy was carrying her baseball glove and a bat. She was wearing her baseball cap. Jason had a glove too, and his new softball.

"Come on," he said to Kristy. "Let's go."

"Just a sec," she replied. Then she told us she was taking Jason to the playground to meet some guys his own age. The playground! It was just like Kristy to come up with an idea like that. A playground was the perfect place to meet kids.

"Bunch of girls," Jason mumbled. "Everywhere we go there are more girls." Jason can be really dumb about stuff.

"Why don't we take Andrew with us?" Mary Anne suggested. "We're checking out some of the stores we missed yesterday. Then we're going to watch the boats in the harbor."

"That'd be great," Kristy told Mary Anne. "Jason and I will catch up with you later. Let's go, Jason."

But Jason was already walking down the street.

"Wait up, Jason," Kristy called as she ran after him.

"Let's go, kids," Mary Anne said to us.

"We are going to the playground, too," I said. I grabbed Martha's hand and yanked her down the street. When we caught up to Kristy she called back to Mary Anne that she would baby-sit for us, and Mary Anne could just take Andrew to the harbor. I wanted to see the boats in the harbor, too. But I knew it was more important to help Martha make friends.

At the playground was a ball field, a playground, and a big barn. A bunch of boys Jason's age were playing softball. And some kids were playing on the slides and the jungle gym. "Jason and I are going to the ballfield," Kristy said. "You girls stay around here." She whispered to me, "Jason wants to meet boys his own age. I need you to stay out of the way for awhile. Okay?"

Martha and I played on the swings, but I kept an eye on how Jason was doing. Kristy was tossing the softball to him. He could catch and hit a softball pretty well. I am on Kristy's softball team so I know a lot about softball. The guys playing in the field were not so good. I could not understand why they did not ask Jason to play. And Kristy, too. She could have helped them have more fun. At home we have much more fun when Kristy plays softball with us than when we try to play games on our own. Maybe Martha could play softball, I thought. Maybe if we started playing with Kristy those other boys would invite us to play with them. And I knew some of those boys must have younger sisters for Martha to meet.

Martha and I were swinging back and forth on the baby swings, pushing sand with our feet. "Martha," I said, "come on. Kristy wants us on the ballfield."

"No, she doesn't," Martha said. "I've been watching."

"She does, too," I said. "I know what Kristy is thinking and she wants to teach you softball. She is my sister and I can read her mind."

"No, you can't," Martha said.

"I can, too. I know she wants us to come over right now and you have to do it because she is our baby-sitter."

"No, I don't," Martha said.

I lost my temper. I could not help it. "You have to because I said so," I yelled. "I need to find some friends for you so you will like to live here. Help a little. Say hi to the people I introduce you to. Look them in the eye. Why do you have to be so shy?" I was so mad I kicked a little sand in her direction.

She kicked more sand back at me. "Why do you have to bug me?" she asked.

"Because I like you," I shouted. I kicked

sand at her again. But the wind blew it back in my face.

"I'm sorry," Martha said.

I thought it was so funny that I kicked the sand and she apologized that I had to giggle. "You did not kick it," I told her. "I did."

"But I kicked sand, too," Martha said. "So I'm sorry."

"Me, too," I said. "I am sorry I yelled."

"Are we still friends?" Martha asked.

"Of course we are."

Martha had a lot to learn about friendship. You can be friends even if you have a fight.

"Come on," I said. "We can help Kristy play ball with Jason."

Martha followed me to the softball field. Jason looked pretty disappointed to see us. Kristy did, too. But sometimes you have to ignore what people think and do what you know is right for your friends. Those other boys were stupid. They did not ask any of us to play ball with them. Even when they saw me play. Which shows you how much they know about softball. Not much.

CHAPTER 9

LOGAN

WEDNESDAY

DEAR MARY ANNE,

    I MISS YOU. A LOT.

    I'M NOT THE ONLY ONE WHO MISSES YOU! WAIT UNTIL I TELL YOU WHAT HAPPENED AT THE BSC MEETING TODAY. FOR ME IT ALL STARTED AFTER THE MEETING, WHEN MALLORY CAME LOOKING FOR ME AT THE ROSEBUD CAFE . . .

The Rosebud Cafe, where I'm working as a busboy, is usually pretty busy. That's why our boss says, "No phone calls or friends dropping by while you're on the job." I made sure to tell this to my friends when I started the job. So I was pretty surprised when a so-called friend of mine — Mallory Pike — burst into the Rosebud on Monday and started trailing me while I cleared tables and served water and bread. And she was yakking a mile a minute!

"Mal, I can't talk now," I hissed at her over my shoulder. "Can't you see that I'm busy?"

"You don't understand, Logan," she insisted. "This is important."

"You can't follow me around, Mal," I insisted. "My boss will have a fit. I'll get fired."

"Okay. I'll stay right here." Mallory stood between the counter, where I pick up water and bread, and the door to the kitchen, where I take trays of dirty dishes. As I made trips back and forth, Mal told me what had happened at the Monday BSC meeting.

I wasn't at the meeting (obviously) and neither was Shannon. It was just Mal and Jessi in Claudia's room. Mal had been acting president and Jessi had been acting secretary.

The first thing Mal and Jessi did was check

the answering machine. But there were no messages.

"Do you think that's because people know that Kristy and the others aren't here?" Jessi asked. "Maybe Jake told all the other kids that they'd get *us* if they called for sitters."

"I don't know," Mal answered. "Maybe."

"How did things go with the twins at the Prezziosos'?"

"I barely survived," Mal told her. "It's the sort of job that would be better with two sitters. I already wrote about it in the notebook." She sighed. "But I'm baby-sitting for them again tomorrow — solo."

Just then the phone rang. Mal looked at the clock and saw that it was exactly five-thirty. The call was from Mrs. Arnold, asking that I (Logan) go to my job (the one I hadn't heard about yet) at her place a few minutes early.

Mal was afraid Mrs. Arnold could hear her voice shaking when she told her, "Sure, Mrs. Arnold. I'll get in touch with Logan right away. He'll be there by seven-fifteen at the latest." When she hung up, Mal asked Jessi, "Did you tell Logan about that job at the Arnolds' tonight?"

"I thought you were going to," Jessi answered.

"I forgot," Mal confessed. "We better call him right away."

Jessi checked the schedule I'd given them and saw that I was working at the Rosebud until six-thirty. "Even though he told us not to, I'm going to call him at the restaurant," Mal said. "It's an emergency."

But before she could pick up the phone, it rang again. This time it was Mal's mother needing a sitter for the next day. Mal told her there were no sitters available. "But I'm one of your oldest and best clients," Mrs. Pike complained, only half-joking. Mallory felt awful about disappointing her mother. But what could she do?

The phone rang again. This time it was a new client who'd heard about the BSC from the Braddocks. "I'm sorry," Mal said, "but we don't have any sitters available tomorrow afternoon. Please call us again."

"Don't forget to call Logan," Jessi reminded Mal. Before Mal could make the call there was a knock on Claud's door. "It's me. Janine." Claudia's sister poked her head in the room.

"We're having a Baby-sitters Club meeting," Jessi told her.

"I need to speak with you," Janine replied.

"When our meeting is over," Mal said. "We have a lot of calls to make."

"More than you think," Janine said.

"What do you mean?" Mal asked.

"First of all, did you know that your answering machine isn't on?"

Mal and Jessi checked the machine and saw that she was right.

"So that's why we didn't have any calls," Jessi said.

"On the contrary," Janine said. "You had numerous calls. On our family phone line. When your answering machine didn't take calls, your clients called us. Here."

She handed Mal six messages. One of them was from Shannon, listing the times when she could baby-sit. It was a short list. All the others were from clients requesting sitters. Just then the phone rang with another client needing a sitter. Mal said she'd call right back.

"Janine," Mal said when she hung up the phone, "um, how would you like to make some extra money?"

Janine agreed to take one job. "I certainly don't want to see the club destroyed because some of its members are on an out-of-town assignment," she said.

The club destroyed? Janine had just put Jessi's and Mal's worst nightmare into words.

"So," Janine continued, "I'll take one night job. But I can't oblige you tonight." She grinned. "Because I have a date."

They gave Janine a job with the Hobarts for the following night.

After she left, the meeting lasted an extra twenty minutes, while Mal and Jessi returned clients' calls. Out of six jobs, they had to turn down four. At that point, Mal told me, they were so desperate for more baby-sitters that they considered calling Stacey McGill, our ex-treasurer, to see if she'd help out.

"We can't ask Stacey to help us," Jessi said. "Even if she said she'd take a job, she might not show up for it. You know she puts Robert before anything else."

"That's what's so great about Mary Anne and Logan," Mal said.

"*Logan,*" they screamed in unison as they remembered that they still hadn't told me about my job with the Arnolds.

"Mal," Jessi said with a gasp, "call him. Quick."

Mal tried calling the Rosebud, but kept getting a busy signal. How could she know that my boss takes the phone off the hook when things are really busy? And believe me, that afternoon we were really busy.

"I better go over there," Mal said. "It's already six-twenty-five."

"Six-twenty-five?" Jessi said. "Oh no! I told

Becca I'd teach her how to Rollerblade at six o'clock. Dinner's at six-thirty and then I'm sitting for Becca and Squirt. My parents and Aunt Cecelia are going to that auction for the Ambulance Squad."

"If there *is* an auction," Mal cried. "I better find Logan fast."

Mal and Jessi had already dashed down the stairs when Jessi remembered the answering machine and ran back to turn it on. By then Mal was jogging toward the Rosebud Cafe.

"But I can't sit tonight, Mal," I said, when she'd finished her tale of woe. I was filling water glasses at the busboy station. "When this shift is over, I'm picking up the night shift. As a favor for a friend."

"How could you?" Mal practically shouted. "Tonight's the night you said you could baby-sit."

"When you guys didn't call with a job, I figured I was free." (Now I was slicing french bread.) "So I told this guy, Carlos, I'd take his shift. You'll have to find someone else to sit."

"There is no one else!" Mal shrieked. She was getting so panicky her face was as red as her hair, and she was moving around like a Mexican jumping bean.

"Mal, quiet down," I said. I picked up another loaf of bread to slice. "Get a grip."

She grabbed the bread from my hand and shook it violently. "You get a grip," she said between clenched teeth. The loaf of bread folded like a rag doll. She continued to shake it at me anyway. "This is important," she hissed. "Mrs. Arnold is running the auction for the ambulance squad. If people die because there's no ambulance, it'll be your fault."

My boss, who was showing customers to a table, looked over to see what the ruckus was about. The other busboy (bus*person*) on the Monday afternoon shift was Geraldine Breslin. She stood in front of Mal so our boss wouldn't see that Mal was mangling his french bread.

When Mal finally stopped to catch her breath, Geraldine whispered, "What's going on here?"

I asked Geraldine if she could do me the humongous favor of taking the shift I'd said I would take for Carlos.

"Please, oh please, please," Mal begged Geraldine. By then Mal was wringing the bread like a handkerchief.

"I guess I better," Geraldine said, "before all we have left to serve the customers are bread crumbs."

MAL — ACTING PRESIDENT OF THE BABY-
SITTERS CLUB — WAS STILL HOLDING
ON TO THAT PATHETIC LOAF OF BREAD
WHEN I RUSHED HER OUT OF THE
RESTAURANT.

"OH, THANK YOU, THANK YOU, LOGAN,"
SHE EXCLAIMED. "YOU'RE A WONDERFUL
GUY. NO WONDER MARY ANNE LOVES
YOU. I LOVE YOU. WE ALL LOVE YOU.
STONEYBROOK AMBULANCE SERVICES
SHOULD NAME AN AMBULANCE AFTER
YOU."

AT THAT MOMENT I WASN'T FEELING
VERY LOVING TOWARD MAL. BUT I LOVE
YOU, MARY ANNE — EVEN IF YOU DO
HAVE SOME GOOFY FRIENDS. I CAN'T
WAIT UNTIL YOU COME HOME.

LOVE,
LOGAN

Dawn

Monday
11 p.m.

Kristy, I know that helping
the Menders kids adjust to
the idea of living in Reese, is
more important than solving
mysteries. But I'm beginning
to think they shouldn't live
in a haunted house. And
this house is definitely,
positively haunted. Yes, some
of the noises we hear at
night are just the creaks of
a big old house. But the
footsteps I heard over my
head a few minutes ago
are <u>footsteps</u>. They couldn't
be anything else! And I

Dawn

also heard an eerie sound in the wall of my bedroom. It sounded like a cry for help. Was it Mary's ghost? Or another ghost?

"**B**ut I don't *want* to meet any other kids," Jill protested. "And I don't want to play with Karen and Martha. They're too young. I want to play — I mean hang around — with you, Dawn."

It was Monday afternoon. Kristy, Jason, and Andrew were at the playground. Mary Anne had taken Martha and Karen shopping. That left Claudia, Jill, and me, swinging in the hammock under the pine trees. Jill and I were watching Claud sketch the mansion, which was mostly a drawing of the widow's walk. I was *desperate* to talk to Claudia about Mary Randolph and Georgio Trono. But Jill was glued to me, as usual. And she had no intention of "playing" with anyone else.

"Where's Spooky?" I asked Jill. "Why don't you play with your cat?"

"Spooky disappeared," she said.

"When did you last see him?" Claudia asked.

"Last night. Before I went to bed. He was in the hall and I said, 'Come on, Spooky, you can sleep in here.' But he ran away from me."

Claudia and I exchanged a look behind Jill's back. We both thought that Spooky was . . . spooky.

"So what have you planned for my entertainment this afternoon?" a booming voice asked. Lionel had snuck up on us. Again.

I jumped so high I almost fell out of the hammock. "Lionel!" I shouted. "Stop sneaking up on us."

"You scare easily," he said. He sat on the ground near us and gave the hammock little pushes.

"So," he said, "what's the plan? Or are the baby-sitters just going to sit around all day?"

"You know what might be fun?" Claudia asked. "We could eat in the dining room tonight. And dress up for dinner."

"Wow! Great! I mean, if you think so, Dawn," said Jill.

"I think that would be great fun," I replied.

"We'll set the table with all the fancy dinnerware that's in the dining room cabinet," Claud continued. "It's probably been in your family for a zillion years, Lionel."

"Some of Uncle Edward's suits are sixty or seventy years old. I saw them in a closet,"

Lionel said. "Maybe I'll wear his tuxedo."

Yes! We'd finally hit on an idea that Lionel liked.

I wished there were some antique women's clothes around, too. We'd have to put together outfits from the clothes we brought. I knew Claud would help us figure out that part. But first we had to get permission from Lionel's parents, and talk to the Coopers.

Mr. and Mrs. Menders thought having a formal dinner was a terrific idea and said they'd be back from their afternoon of research in plenty of time to "dress for dinner."

Claud, Lionel, Jill, and I went to the kitchen to talk to the Coopers. Elton said they'd be glad to make a special dinner. They'd been hoping for an opportunity to serve on the good china. Margaret beamed her big smile and rubbed her hands together as if she couldn't wait to start cooking something fancy.

"You see to setting the table and we'll see to the cooking," Elton told us.

"And of course we'll help clean up after dinner," Claud said.

In the dining room we set out the fancy dishes, silverware, and crystal that we'd seen in the cabinet. Lionel opened the french doors to the veranda to air the room out, and we set to work. I read the directions on the silver polish bottle and showed Jill what to do. Claud and Lionel went to the kitchen to wash and dry the crystal glasses.

"Everyone gets two glasses," Claud said when she returned with a tray of sparkling glasses.

"Two forks and three spoons," I added.

Mrs. Cooper brought us a linen tablecloth and napkins. Finally, we were ready to set the table. On the dishes was a delicate, hand-painted rose pattern.

"Some of the roses that Georgio planted look just like these," Claud said. (She looked pretty dreamy when she said that.) Then she had a very Claud idea. "Let's make place-cards," she said. "I can copy the rose pattern from the dishes."

That's when Lionel announced that he'd had his fill of our afternoon project and went off to his room.

When we'd finished setting the table I stepped back to take a look. "You know what we're missing?" I said. "A candelabra."

"There's one," Jill said. She was pointing to the top shelf in the cabinet. I found a stool in the kitchen and climbed up to check out the candelabra.

As I took it down I could see that it needed a good cleaning. It wasn't dusty, but whoever used it last hadn't cleaned off the wax drippings.

I handed it to Claudia before I stepped off the stool. "That's interesting," Claud said. "The wax on here is orange."

"Why is that interesting?" Jill asked.

I gave Claud a Look over Jill's head. "Because people don't use orange candles that much," I said.

"I saw some pink candles in a drawer in the cabinet," Claud said. "We'll use those."

While I cleaned and polished the candelabra, Jill and Claud made placecards.

"Wouldn't it be great if we could have some of the roses from the garden for the table?" Claud said.

The moment she said that, Georgio walked through the french doors. He was carrying the most beautiful bouquet of roses I'd ever seen. "I thought you might like these for your dinner party," he said as he handed them to Claudia. "There's one rose from each of the bushes I planted this morning."

I could tell Claudia was rattled. I was, too. First of all, the instant Claudia said she wanted roses, Georgio appeared with them. Secondly, he knew we were having a dinner party and we hadn't told him. Maybe Elton had told him, but still it *felt* weird.

116

Georgio admired the way we'd set the table. "If you need candles," he said, "I have some in the shed. They're orange, though. Maybe they wouldn't go."

"We don't want orange candles," Jill said. "We're using pink."

"Whatever Claudia thinks will look best, will definitely look best," Georgio said. "She has great taste." Then he left the way he had come. Through the french doors.

Hmmm. If Georgio was our "ghost" the first night, he sure wasn't trying to keep his orange candles a secret.

By the way, I was right about Claud helping us with clothes. She had brought *two* long skirts. So I wore one with my pink tank top and Claud's long rope of fake pearls. Jill wore a skirt of mine, which was long on her. ("I want to dress just like you, Dawn.") I fixed my hair — and Jill's — in french braids. Kristy and Mary Anne, who might not ordinarily be too excited about dressing for dinner, got in the mood when they saw all the work we'd done in the dining room.

"It's so elegant!" Mary Anne said.

"This is great," Kristy added.

"Oh goody, goody, triple goody," Karen exclaimed. "We can be Lovely Ladies! Come on, Martha. We have to look through my mother's clothes. And your mother's. And we can wear makeup and jewelry and high heels." She grabbed Martha's hand, and they ran from the room.

"Uh-oh," Kristy said as she headed after them.

By seven o'clock we were sipping fizzy punch "cocktails" in the parlor. Lionel and Claudia were helping the Coopers in the kitchen and dining room with last-minute details. A bell rang. The doors between the parlor and dining room opened, and Lionel and Claud appeared, Lionel looking spiffy in his great-uncle's tux, Claud looking amazing in a full-length black gauze skirt over a black leotard. She was wearing dangling glass earrings that she'd made from an old chandelier. Her long black hair was held back on one side with a single red rose.

Lionel bowed like a butler. "Ladies and gentlemen," he announced, "dinner is served."

The dinner was delicious. We started with an appetizer of fancy bite-sized pizzas. Then we had a green salad followed by a main course of roasted chicken and mashed potatoes. While we were eating our elegant dessert (ice cream with caramel sauce and wafer thin cookies), Mr. Menders tapped his glass. "I'd like to make a toast," he said.

We lifted our glasses. "First, I want to thank you all for this lovely party. Second, I want to say that our plan to set up a business here is coming along well. We have a lot more research to do, but things are looking good. We may very well be able to move to Reese permanently."

"DAD!" Lionel shouted (in his *own* voice). "How can you say that, when you promised us we'd have a say in the decision? That it was our decision too? Reese is the most boring place in the world? I won't be able to pursue my acting career here. I for one *do not want to move to Reese*. Period. The end."

"I don't like it either," Jason said. "The kids are stuck-up."

Mr. and Mrs. Menders looked discouraged. "What about you, Martha?" Mrs. Menders asked.

"I want to go back to Boston." Martha had to say it twice before her mother could hear her. But I heard it the first time.

"And I want to move to Stoneybrook in the house right next to Dawn's," said Jill.

Kristy, Claud, Mary Anne, and I looked helplessly at one another. We were supposed to be helping the kids adjust. So far we hadn't done a very good job.

That night the parents said they'd put their

119

own kids to bed while my friends and I helped
in the kitchen. There were a lot of dishes to
do, and we had to be extremely careful because everything was antique, and some of it
was fragile.

While Kristy and Mary Anne cleared the
table, Claud and I washed the dishes from the
first course and Mr. and Mrs. Cooper put away
their cooking utensils and generally cleaned
up.

"So," Mr. Cooper said, "are you girls still
thinking about the lights you saw on the
fourth floor?"

"Yes," Claud admitted. "But there's something else."

She told the Coopers what we had learned
about Reginald and Mary Randolph at the library. Then she asked, "Was that the story
you didn't want to tell us last night?"

"No," Elton said. "Though of course I knew
about Mary Randolph's terrible grief and tragic
end. I was thinking of — "

Mrs. Cooper banged her hand on the table
and shook her head no. Mr. Cooper said,
"Now, Margaret, these girls are mature
enough to handle a little history. They're interested in the mansion, and Lydia is part of
the story."

"Who's Lydia?" I asked.

By then Mary Anne and Kristy had returned with trays of dirty dishes. So all four of us were there when Elton told us about Lydia Randolph.

"Lydia Randolph was the grandaughter of Reginald and Mary Randolph," he began. "I hear tell that Lydia was a beautiful dark-haired young woman who was having a romance with the gardener's son. He was a handsome youth named George, who worked on the estate as a groom in the stables. Lydia's paternal grandparents were dead by then. It was her parents who found out about the romance and forbade her to see George again. To that end, they fired both George and his father and forced the entire family to leave the estate. But George secretly returned. Lydia's parents found her with him in the gardener's cottage.

"Her parents locked Lydia in one of the back bedrooms on the fourth floor. She was a prisoner in her own home. The seasons passed. Then a year passed. And another. And another. Until five years had passed and that poor girl was still imprisoned.

"During those years George had made a career for himself and a small fortune. It was all done so that he might convince the Randolphs that he was worthy of their daughter. But when George returned to Reese as a successful businessman, the Randolphs would not receive him and repeatedly ordered him turned away. Where, George wondered, was Lydia? Had she married another? Had she died? Finally a servant told George that his beloved was imprisoned on the fourth floor.

"George could not rest until he found a way to free Lydia. Finally he managed to make his way to the fourth floor. Some say he built a secret passage, but I've not seen one. Anyway, he did get up there. But he couldn't find Lydia. There was only one person on the fourth floor, a white-haired old woman living in one of the back rooms.

" 'Where's my Lydia?' he asked the old woman.

" 'I am Lydia,' she answered."

I gasped. So did Claud. Mary Anne turned so pale I was afraid she'd faint.

"Tragic," Elton said. "Terribly tragic."

"What happened next?" I asked him in a whisper.

"I don't know. But strange things happened on these old estates. So don't let it scare you."

"But this happened here," Claud murmured fearfully.

"Well, that's all very interesting," Kristy told Elton. Then she said to us, "Let's finish up in here. I'm calling an emergency BSC

122

meeting. Since Andrew is sleeping in my room we'll meet in Mary Anne's room in half an hour."

I couldn't wait to be alone with my friends to talk about Lydia Randolph. Which is exactly what Claudia and I were doing when we walked into Mary Anne's room for the meeting thirty minutes later.

I sat on the bed next to Mary Anne. "It was so creepy," I said with a shudder.

Kristy came in right behind me and announced, "I call this emergency meeting of the Baby-sitters Club to order."

When everyone was quiet I said, "You guys, did you notice that Lydia's boyfriend's name was *George* and he was the *gardener's* son? And her name was Lydia which sounds a lot like Claudia."

"It's all too weird," Claudia said.

But Kristy didn't want to hear anything about mysteries or ghosts. "I repeat," she said sternly, "I call this emergency meeting of the Baby-sitters Club to order."

"Isn't the meeting about what Elton just told us?" I asked.

"It certainly is not," Kristy answered. "We're having this meeting to talk about the kids. We're not doing a very good job. It's our responsibility to help the kids adjust, and clearly they are not adjusting. Did you hear what they said at dinner? None of them is happy here. Not one of them."

Kristy was right. So for the rest of the meeting we talked about the kids. My main concern was how to persuade Jill to spend time with someone besides me. "If only she'd play with Martha," I said. "I have to find something that they both love to do and make them do it together."

Claudia had an idea about how we might help Lionel. "Wednesday is our night off," she said. "Let's invite Lionel to go out for pizza with us, and then we'll go to the summer stock play. It'll be our treat."

"And while we're at the play, we'll make sure he meets some of the people who work there," I added. "Especially kids his age."

"You mean we're going to see *Dracula*?" Mary Anne asked. "I don't know." She shivered.

But we all knew it was the best thing we could do for Lionel. And what was best for the Menders kids had to be our main concern.

At the end of the meeting we returned to our rooms. Since Claud hadn't slept very well on my floor the night before, she decided to sleep in her own room that night. If we were going to be first-rate sitters the next day, we needed our sleep.

Even when I heard the footsteps above me, I stayed in my room. And when I heard that eerie cry in the wall, I stayed in my room, too. I was so terrified, so petrified, that I probably couldn't have moved if I'd wanted to.

I tried writing in the BSC Reese notebook for awhile. But I couldn't write about the kids. All I could think about was ghosts. Finally I worked up the nerve to turn off the light. I lay there, staring into the dark.

Then my heart stopped. Absolutely stopped. I heard the very last thing I wanted to hear: the sound of my door creaking open. I reached for the light, but before I could find the switch, something landed on my legs. I screamed. I turned on the light. It was Spooky. The cat sat on my stomach and stared into my eyes. I could barely breathe. When I looked away from him I saw a white-robed figure standing in my doorway. Who — or what — was coming toward me? I tried to scream again but, just the way it happens in nightmares, no sound came out.

That was when I realized it was Jill walking into my room. She was wearing a long white nightgown. Phew. Spooky jumped off the bed and bounded out of the room. I drew a deep, shaky breath.

"I found Spooky under my bed, Dawn," Jill said. "I wanted to tell you. But he jumped out of my arms and you scared him away again."

I scared *him*?

I finally found my voice. "Sh-sh," I told Jill. "We'll wake the others." I climbed out of bed. "Come on. I'll take you back to your room."

I turned on all the lights in my room and the one in the hall. And I made sure to close my door behind me. I didn't want anyone — or any*thing* — coming in while I was gone.

CHAPTER 11

Mary Anne

Tuesday
2:00 p.m.

I loved going through all the old things in the attic this morning. Sometimes I daydream about how it would have been to live in a town like Reese a hundred years ago. Actually, it's hard to think of anything but ghosts right now, but I'm trying. Really, there has to be some logical explanation for everything that's happening here.

Mary Anne

"There go our outdoor plans for the kids," Kristy said.

We were in her room helping Andrew get dressed for the day. A rainy day.

"Boats," Andrew said. "Kristy, I want to go see the boats again."

Kristy handed Andrew a pair of clean socks. "Today you can draw pictures of boats," she told him.

Dawn, Claudia, and Jill burst into the room then.

"I know the perfect rainy day activity," Claudia announced. "We can explore the attic."

"That's a super idea!" I exclaimed. "I bet there's a lot of stuff up there."

"And we can make an inventory for the Menderses," Kristy suggested. "The contents of the attic are part of their inheritance."

"What about what Georgio said?" I asked.

"He was just trying to scare us," Claud said. "Don't worry about it."

"I bet there'll be some wonderful old things up there," I said.

"Like old photo albums," Dawn said.

"And antique clothes," Claud added. "We might find some ideas and costumes for our float."

128

At breakfast Seth and Lisa and the Menderses told us that their plan for the day was to visit the business district in Reese and a couple of nearby towns to make a study of how many people shopped on a rainy summer day. When we told them *our* plan, they agreed that it was a perfect rainy day activity.

"There's just one problem," Claudia said. "The door to the staircase that leads to the fourth floor is locked."

"I know," Mr. Menders said. He told us that he'd been up on the top floor once, when he surveyed the house after the reading of his uncle's will. "But after that," he said, "the key disappeared."

"And the Coopers' set of keys doesn't have one either," Mrs. Menders added.

Mr. Menders handed Claud his set of keys. "Give my keys one more try," he said. "If none of them works for you either, ask Elton to break the lock. We'll have to go up there sooner or later."

"What's the fourth floor like?" Dawn asked.

"Well, as you know," Mr. Menders answered, "the stairs begin in your third floor hallway. At the top of the stairs to the right is a door to the attic. To the left is a hallway with bedrooms off of it. I only went into a couple of them. It's pretty obvious that they haven't been used in generations."

While the rest of the sitters and kids searched through old bureau drawers and cabinets for the missing key, Claud and I ran upstairs and tried all the keys on Mr. Menders's keyring. He was right. None of them worked.

By then Kristy, Dawn, and the kids had brought us the handful of keys they'd found around the house. While Claud tried those, I returned to my room to find a pad and pen for making a list of the contents of the attic. When I looked out my window to see if the rain was slowing down, I noticed Georgio working in one of the gardens. I thought it was strange for him to be working outside in a heavy downpour. I thought it was even stranger that he wasn't paying much attention to his work. He kept glancing up at the mansion, as if he were looking for something — or someone. I backed away from the window. I didn't want him to see me. I had a feeling that Georgio was spying on us.

I found a notebook and a pen and headed back to the locked door where Kristy was saying, "I'll go ask Mr. Cooper to break the lock."

"Can I help you with something?" a male voice asked.

Claud jumped about a mile, and I yelped.

It was Georgio. He seemed to have appeared out of nowhere.

"Sorry I scared you," he said. "I just wondered if I could help."

What was he doing in the house? How did he know we needed help?

"We are going to explore the attic," Karen said. "But we cannot get in."

"I really don't think you should go up there," Georgio replied.

"Mr. and Mrs. Menders told us we could," Claud said.

"My dad lost the key," Jill added.

"Do *you* have a key?" Karen asked.

Georgio hesitated a second. Then he said quietly, "I might."

"Then try to open the door for us," Kristy said. "Please."

Georgio took a set of keys from his belt. He selected a key and easily unlocked the door with it.

"Oh, goody," Karen said. "You are our hero."

I didn't think Georgio was a hero. I was just about convinced he was our fourth-floor "ghost."

Before he left us Georgio said, "Be careful. If you need me for anything I'll be in the garden. You can call me from the window."

Mary Anne

As we climbed the stairs I felt as afraid of Georgio as I did of the attic. But after the first few minutes up there I was so interested and busy that for a while I forgot about being afraid.

The attic was everything we had hoped it would be — and more. I was so busy writing down what everyone else was finding, that at first I didn't make any discoveries myself. But I did see a lot of wonderful antiques.

Here are just some of the things we found:

sewing form (woman)
sewing form (man)
antique baby carriage
2 sleds
trunk of baby clothes
hundreds of old magazines
two photo albums
trunk of children's toys
2 rocking chairs
croquet set
large armoire (clothes closet)

While Kristy and Jason pawed through the trunk of toys with the younger children, the rest of us continued the survey of the attic.

I tested the handle of the armoire. "It isn't locked," I told Dawn. "But I'm afraid to open it. There might be bats in there." I backed up while Lionel pulled the doors open. Of course he had to say something about bats and Dracula while he did it. "Don't you know, my dear, that we sleep in our coffins during the day? Not in some dusty old cupboard."

There were no bats in the armoire. It wasn't dusty either. It held three white cotton garment bags. Two were snapped closed, but the middle one was open. We looked inside the open bag first. It held two gowns. One was yellow satin with a smocked bodice. The other was dark blue velvet with black lace trim. I inspected the smocking and handmade lace. "The handiwork on these is amazing," I told the others. "It's so intricate." (I love to do what Claud calls "the sewing arts." I've learned how to embroider, smock, and make quilts.)

Claud and Dawn opened the other two garment bags. All the gowns were distinctive and beautiful.

"Oh, I wish we'd found these before our dress-up dinner!" exclaimed Claudia.

"Why are there three gowns in each of these bags," Dawn wondered out loud, "but only two in the middle one?"

"Maybe there were only eight gowns to put away," I said.

"Then why wasn't the bag closed?" Dawn asked. "Whoever put these gowns away was very careful with the others."

Claud looked around to be sure the kids couldn't hear her when she asked, "Do you think these were Lydia's gowns?"

But Lionel heard her. "Lydia," he intoned. "Oh, my beloved Lydia. They can't separate us. I will rescue you. A team of wild horses couldn't keep me away from you."

When he finished his performance, Dawn asked him, "How'd you know about Lydia?"

"Elton told me. I assume that's who told you."

"He told me, too," Jill piped up.

I was surprised that Mr. Cooper had told Jill the story of Lydia. I thought that was a pretty scary story to tell a kid.

"It's probably not true," I said. "Sometimes people make up a story, like on Halloween, and the people who hear it think it's true."

"I don't care," Jill said. "Dawn and I don't scare easy. Do we, Dawn?"

Dawn just sighed.

While Dawn and Claudia snapped the garment bags closed, I peered in the toy box. I wanted to include some of the larger toys on my list. "What did you guys find?" I asked.

"Stuff you'd love," Kristy responded. "They're ancient."

"We have to be very careful with these toys," Karen said, holding up an antique porcelain doll, "because they might be worth a lot of money."

Andrew showed me a faded red wooden boat about the size of a loaf of bread. "This is my boat," he said. "I like boats."

Kristy explained to Andrew that he could play with the boat while we were in the attic, but that it wasn't his, and it would have to go back into the trunk.

The next big discovery of the morning was two photo albums in the drawer of the armoire. Claud opened one book to a black and white photo of a beautiful young woman. "I bet this is Lydia," she said. I recognized the woman's dress. It was the satin gown with the smocked bodice. Looking at that picture gave me chills.

The photo albums were fascinating. I loved seeing the way people dressed, and how Reese looked so long ago.

"This guy looks so much like somebody I know," Claud said. She was pointing to a photo of a middle-aged man. He had on one of those stiff pointy collars men used to wear in the early nineteen hundreds.

"Someone in Stoneybrook?" I asked.

"Maybe," Claud answered. "I wish I could figure out who." She turned the page. "It'll come to me later."

"I'm sick of being up here," I heard Jason complain to Kristy. "All we're doing is looking at old toys and *dresses*."

Kristy glanced out the attic window. "The rain's letting up a little, Jason," she said. "After lunch maybe you and I can head over to that playground."

"Martha and me, too," Karen said.

"Karen, you can do something with the others this afternoon," Kristy said in her I-mean-what-I-say voice. "Jason and I are going alone this time."

"Oh, boo," Karen said. "Boo, boo, and triple boo."

Just then I felt a gentle tap on my arm. It was Dawn. "Mary Anne," she whispered to me, "before we go back downstairs, Claud and I are going to try to figure out which bedroom was Lydia's."

"And find the stairs to the widow's walk," Claud added.

I couldn't imagine doing such an unbearably scary thing.

"Do you want to come with us?" Dawn asked.

"No, I do not," I said emphatically. "And I don't want you to go either. Please, let's all go back downstairs together."

"We'll be down in a minute," Dawn said. But I noticed she didn't look too relaxed herself. She and Claud headed down the hall while Kristy and I took the kids downstairs. Kristy continued with the kids to the first floor while I waited in our hall for Dawn and Claud. I was wondering how they could do such a scary thing, when suddenly I heard feet running along the floor above me. Did they belong to two people? Or to two people being chased by a third? What if our villain were chasing Claud and Dawn?

Footsteps were pounding down the stairs. Even though I was terrified I opened the door to the stairwell. Dawn and Claud practically tumbled down the last few stairs. As soon as they were in the hall I banged the door shut.

"What did you see?" I managed to say.

"The cat's up there," Claud answered. "At first we thought it was a person . . . or ghost."

"I think that cat *is* a ghost," Dawn said.

"Or belongs to one," Claud added.

We shuddered.

"But we had time to figure out that the doors

to the widow's walk and to the bedrooms on the back side of the house, including the one that was Lydia's, are locked," Dawn said.

I couldn't help wondering if Georgio had keys to those rooms, too.

CHAPTER 12

Kristy

Tuesday
11:45 p.m.

I really meant what I said last night at our emergency BSC meeting. We have to forget about ghost-busting and focus on our baby-sitting job. If we spend our nights worrying about ghosts, it's going to be harder and harder to spend our days taking care of kids. (I am already exhausted.) But here I am tonight, wide awake and scared out of my wits again.

"Come on, Jason, grab your glove. We're going to the playground." It was after lunch on Tuesday and I was determined to help Jason Menders meet some guys his own age.

"But it's still raining," he protested.

"So we'll see what the kids do here on a rainy day. I bet they're in the recreation barn."

"I don't want to go," Jason said. "Those guys are stuck-up."

"Would you rather stay here and play dress-up with Karen and Martha?" I asked.

That did it. Jason ran upstairs and returned with his glove. "Let's go to the playground," he said.

The rain was still coming down hard when we reached the playground. No one was outside, so we headed for the rec barn. It was kind of small — about the size of a two-car garage.

I was happy to see that the place was filled with the guys we'd seen playing softball the day before. Four of them were playing Ping-Pong. They looked at us when we came in, but didn't say hi or anything. Another group was sitting on an old couch playing a hand-held computer game. More kids were sitting at a table playing a board game.

Not one kid greeted us. Also, they didn't seem to be having much fun. I figured they were sick of being cooped up because of the rain.

"Do you know how to play Ping-Pong?" I whispered to Jason.

"There's a Ping-Pong table in the cellar of my building in Boston," Jason whispered back. "I'm the best player on the block."

"Okay," I said. "Ask them if you can play."

"I can't do THAT!" Jason hissed.

"Of course you can!"

Jason turned his baseball cap backward, handed me his glove and ball, and walked to the Ping-Pong table. "Can I play the winner?" he asked. I was so proud of him.

But no one would have been proud of those other kids. "We're not playing for points," one of them said. Not another word out of any of them. They kept hitting that Ping-Pong ball back and forth, back and forth, and ignoring Jason.

It was time for more aggressive action. I walked over to the table. "Hi," I said, "I'm Kristy Thomas."

"And I'm Jason Menders," Jason said.

None of them said a word to us. But I heard a boy behind me say, "The summer boy has a *nanny*." I was glad Jason was on the other side of the Ping-Pong table and didn't hear that comment.

"I coach a softball team in Stoneybrook, Connecticut," I announced to anyone who would listen. "I wish my team was in Reese with me, because if they were I'd challenge you guys to a game. Who's your coach?"

"Our coach is gone," a red-haired kid muttered. "He went to be a counselor at a sleep-away camp."

"Oh. I guess if he were around he'd be able to help you guys with that problem you have making the double play."

"And your hitting," Jason added.

"What's the matter with our hitting?" a tough-looking kid asked.

I dodged his question by saying, "I guess you're not playing in a league or anything if you don't have a coach."

"And I noticed you only have one pitcher," Jason added. (He was doing great!)

"Our other pitcher went to sleepaway camp, too," one of the computer game kids muttered.

"And Chad was no help," the red-haired kid said.

"Who's Chad?" I asked.

"He was our best pitcher last summer. But he's a summer kid. They all leave in Septem-

ber. And September's when the regional softball playoff is. We lost last year 'cause Chad
wasn't here. So we don't play with summer
people or tourists anymore. It's our rule."

I began to get the picture. These guys were
avoiding Jason because they thought he was
one of those "summer people" who leave in
September (and have nannies).

"I might move here," Jason told them. "If
I like it. My uncle died and left us his house."

"Yeah?" one of the Ping-Pong players asked.
"You'd go to school here and everything?"

"Sure," Jason answered. "If I like it."

"I'm not moving here like Jason," I said.
"But I'll be around for another week. Then I
have to go back to my own softball team. My
team is called the Krushers. What's your team
called?"

"We don't have a name," the red-haired kid
said.

"That's too bad," I told him. "I guess you
don't have T-shirts either."

"Who'd want to sponsor *us*?" I heard one
guy whisper to another.

I looked out the window. The rain was letting up.

I tossed Jason his glove across the Ping-Pong
table. I made sure it was a toss he would really
have to reach for. He caught it back-handed.

And all those guys saw him do it.

"I watched you play yesterday. And you know what I saw?" I asked them.

All eyes were on me. No one was pretending to play a game. No one was hitting a Ping-Pong ball. Finally I had their undivided attention. I said, "I saw a lot of talent on that field. As a matter of fact I saw so much talent that I want to help you. I'm willing to help you." For good measure I added, "For free."

They looked at one another. These guys needed a leader so badly they couldn't pull it together to turn me down — even though I'm a girl and they were the kind of boys who'd ordinarily have trouble with that. Which, of course, made me want to play ball with them more than ever. "I'm glad you agree," I told them. "You won't regret it. Let's start by getting out on that muddy field and playing some ball."

There was a chorus of "yeahs" and "okays" as kids grabbed gloves and bats and hustled out the door.

Jason flashed me a thank-you smile as we followed them.

That night, after the kids were asleep, Claudia and Dawn came into my room. Dawn said, "We have an idea about how to clear up the mystery of the ghosts once and for all."

"But we need your help," Claud said. "And Mary Anne's."

When I heard their idea I thought we might be able to put an end to the ghost talk that very night. It sounded dangerous. But I agreed to it. (Mistake #1!)

Mary Anne and I were supposed to go outside at nine-thirty and watch the mansion to see if the fourth-floor lights went on again. Meanwhile, Claudia and Dawn would be spying in the fourth floor hall to see if anyone else (meaning the one person who has a key to the fourth floor — Georgio) came upstairs.

When nine-thirty arrived, Mary Anne and I were hidden behind some bushes. We had a perfect view of the back of the mansion.

"I could never in a million years do what Dawn and Claud are doing," Mary Anne told me. "I'd have a heart attack from fear." (Mistake #2 was thinking that our job wasn't as scary as Claud's and Dawn's.)

Later Claud told us that she and Dawn were both terrified as they went upstairs. What if someone — or some*thing* — were already up there? But they peeked around the corner into the hallway and didn't see anyone. So far, the coast was clear.

"I wish Lydia's room weren't locked," Dawn whispered to Claudia.

"We could peek through the keyhole," Claud said.

Dawn volunteered to do the peeking.

The keyhole provided Dawn with a view of the room. She took a quick look around and reported to Claud, "No one's there, unless they're in the closet."

Claud and Dawn hid themselves in the hallway alcove and waited to see if anyone went in, or out of, that room.

Meanwhile Mary Anne was keeping an eye on the back door to see if anyone went into the house. And I was watching the row of bedroom windows on the fourth floor. Suddenly I saw a light go on in the same room in which I'd seen it the night before. "Mary Anne," I whispered. "Look."

The light stayed on for about two minutes and then went off. During the time it was on we checked to see if it was caused by a reflection from the lighthouse beam. But it was a clear night and the lighthouse was dark. Besides, the light in Lydia's room looked identical to the warm glow given off by all the other electric lights in the house.

We stood still and clutched one another while we watched that window. The light went back on after a couple of minutes. A few minutes later it went off again.

Mary Anne was whispering, "Where are Dawn and Claud? Oh, Kristy, I'm so *worried*." I tried to calm her down but I was pretty scared myself, and I think she could tell.

When the light had stayed off for five minutes, we decided it was time to go in and tell Claud and Dawn what we'd seen. "I hope Georgio didn't find them spying on him," Mary Anne whispered to me as we walked toward the house. A moment later, Mary Anne cried out and hid her face in one hand while she pointed to the top of the mansion with the other. "Tell me I didn't see that," she mumbled into my sweatshirt.

I saw a figure in white walking on the widow's walk. I knew I saw it. It wasn't my imagination. Even after the ghostly figure had disappeared, I was shaking with fright.

"It's gone," I told Mary Anne.

I grabbed her hand and we ran all the way to the mansion and into the kitchen. Elton was sitting at the table reading the newspaper. He looked up and asked, "What's wrong, girls? You look like you've seen a ghost."

"We didn't," I said quickly. "We're in a hurry." It wasn't until later that I wondered why I didn't tell him that we *had* seen a ghost.

We raced up the stairs to the third floor. I was terrified. If Georgio were trying to scare us, he was going to a lot of trouble to do it. What else would he do? How dangerous was he? Then again, if the ghosts were real (which I didn't *truly* believe), they were probably evil ghosts. Dangerous ghosts.

When we saw Dawn and Claud in our hall we all hugged. Dawn and Claudia were pale. We all rushed off to Mary Anne's room to talk. Mary Anne started crying, I guess with relief that they (and we) were safe.

First I told Claud and Dawn about the figure in white. Then we went over everything that had happened, step by step. Claud and Dawn had also seen the light in the room. The hall was dark, so the light glowed through the keyhole. (They were both too frightened to actually look in the keyhole.)

"It's Lydia's room," Claud said. "I just know it. And I'm pretty sure Georgio isn't responsible for any of this. We would have seen him."

"Unless he was hiding in a closet in the room," Dawn said.

"What about the figure in white?" Claud asked. "Georgio couldn't have been in both places at once."

"Maybe he has a woman accomplice,"

148

Dawn suggested. "Kristy said the figure in white looked like a woman."

I could tell that Claud was hoping with all her heart that Georgio wasn't our villain. And she probably didn't want to hear that he had a female accomplice. Poor Claud.

We were so frightened that we whispered our good nights.

A little later, while I was trying to fall asleep, I went over the day's — and night's — events and asked myself questions. What would happen next? Who was doing all these creepy things? And most mysterious of all, why?

The wind — or was it a ghost? — rattled the window.

I lay awake listening to my heartbeat. Finally, I closed my eyes and tried to fall asleep.

I soon felt a thump on my legs. I opened my eyes and stared into yellow-green eyes. I thought of Dracula, and bats, and stories I'd heard of campers waking up to find a snake crawling over them. As my eyes became used to the darkness I was sure a big bat was sitting on my legs. But when the "bat" hss-sshed, and jumped over me and off the bed, I realized it was Spooky.

I saw him run through the bathroom toward Mary Anne's room. I jumped out of bed and followed him. If Spooky did to Mary Anne what he had just done to me, she *definitely* would have a heart attack.

I opened the door onto the hall, hoping Spooky would leave. He did. Then I checked to be sure that Mary Anne was still asleep. She was. But it was a very long time before I fell asleep.

CHAPTER 13

Mallory

Jessi and I are booked solid. Sorry, guys, but we had to turn down quite a few jobs — eight, to be exact. That was on Monday. Today, Wednesday, not many people called.

We miss you all and can't wait until you come home and things go back to normal.

"Mal, I don't feel like being president to-day," Jessi told me. "You can do it."

We were in Claud's room for our Wednes-day BSC meeting, and we were pretty tired from all the baby-sitting we'd been doing. We were the *only* ones at the meeting. Shannon had a dentist appointment and Logan was working at the Rosebud.

"I don't want to be president either," I said. "Since there're only two of us, we don't really need one."

Jessi agreed with a nod. "Let's take turns making calls to the people who left messages," she suggested.

"Sure," I said.

I pressed the play button. I had a piece of paper and a pencil ready to write down the names and phone numbers of callers. But that wasn't necessary for the first message. It was from Jessi.

"This is me — Jessi — just making sure the machine is on and working."

"That was a good idea," I told her. My mood picked up a little. Maybe we weren't doing so badly after all.

"Thanks," Jessi said.

"Beep. Beep. Beep." Three beeps meant there were no more messages.

"I guess my message was the only one," Jessi concluded glumly.

I sat next to her on the bed. "Look at the bright side," I said. "We won't have to turn down so many people."

"Maybe they're waiting until the meeting to call," Jessi suggested.

But fifteen minutes passed and the phone didn't ring once.

"Nothing seems right since the others left," Jessi said. "I'm tired from so many baby-sitting jobs. And Becca is sulking because I don't have time to teach her how to Rollerblade."

"My mom is really grumpy with me, too," I told Jessi. "I explained that it's not my fault that all the sitters left town. But she said we should have planned better. I promised her I'd take all my brothers and sisters to Celebrate America! Day."

Jessi and I were looking forward to Celebrate America! It was Stoneybrook's big summer celebration, starting with a parade in the morning followed by a barbecue picnic at the playground. During the afternoon there'd be games from colonial times, and hands-on activities, such as kite making.

Jessi looked at the record book. "But you're scheduled to take the Rodowskys to Celebrate America!"

"Mrs. Rodowsky is going to be at the fair running the dunking booth, and my mother will be at the kite booth. Since they'll be there, they decided it was okay for me to watch all the kids. I just have to keep ten kids safe and happy!" It sounded like a tough job even if Mrs. Rodowsky and my mom were going to be there.

"I'd help you, but I'm overbooked, too," Jessi said. "I'm going to take the Braddocks, the Marshalls, *and* Becca. Mrs. Braddock and my mother are working together on the make-your-own rag doll booth. So there'll be a lot of adults around that we know. But it's still a huge amount of work."

The BSC phone finally rang.

It was Mrs. Prezzioso wanting a sitter on Celebrate America! Day for Jenny, Andrea, and the twins.

I looked at the list of times Shannon and Logan were available to take jobs. Neither of them had listed that day.

"Sorry, Mrs. Prezzioso," I said. "There aren't any sitters available."

When I hung up I told Jessi, "You know what Mrs. Prezzioso said? 'But I thought the point of the club was to have sitters *available*. I'm very disappointed.'"

"I guess a lot of people are disappointed in

us," Jessi said with a sigh. "What are we going to do, Mal? We've ruined the club."

"Maybe we should make posters and put them up around town," I said. "Or send a letter to our clients."

"By the time they get the letter Kristy and everybody will be home and things will be back to normal," Jessi pointed out.

"Or ruined forever," I added darkly.

"We could put posters up right away," Jessi said.

We talked about the poster idea, but eventually realized that it would be too hard to explain what had happened to the BSC in a few words.

As we left Claud's room I remembered all the wonderful meetings we'd been to there. This hadn't been one of them. Would we ever have good meetings again? Or had we ruined the BSC forever?

CHAPTER 14

Mary Anne

Wednesday
5:00 p.m.

I don't believe in ghosts.
And I don't believe this
mansion is haunted. I
do believe that if we are
thorough in our inves-
tigation (and don't jump
to conclusions) we will
figure out what's really
going on here.

Mary Anne

"**M**ary Anne, take me to see the boats now. Puh-lease."

I opened my eyes. It was Wednesday morning and Andrew had climbed onto my bed to wake me up.

"Oh, goody, you're awake," he said. "Kristy's asleep and I want to see the boats. Okay?"

"Is it a sunny day?" I asked, rubbing my eyes.

"Very sunny," he answered. "There'll be *lots* of boats. This many." He held up both hands to show me his ten fingers.

I explained to Andrew that our day's plan was to spend as much time as we could outdoors, starting at the community swimming pool. "After that we'll go to the harbor and see the boats. But first we'll swim. Okay?"

"I can swim," Andrew said. "I pretend I'm a boat."

I gave him a hug. Andrew's a great kid.

Jill and Dawn came into the room. "We have our swimsuits on under our shorts and T-shirts," Jill informed me. "And we both have on blue T-shirts, see?"

I reminded myself that we *had* to help Jill make some friends her own age in Reese.

After breakfast Kristy and Jason headed off

157

to the ballfield. Lionel said he'd stay home and read *Dracula* (the novel by Bram Stoker). He wanted to read the novel before he saw the play. The rest of us walked the half mile to Reese community pool. It was a huge pool near the ocean. That morning the pool was divided in half with a buoy rope. One half was reserved for the members of the swim team who were waiting poolside in their matching navy and white suits. The other half of the pool was open for general free swim. There was also a kiddie pool, which was perfect for Andrew-the-Boat.

I thought if both Jill and Martha signed up for the swim team, they'd be involved in an activity they could share while meeting kids their own age.

"Girls," I said, "let's go check out the swim team."

"Martha, *you* should be on the swim team," Karen exclaimed. "I bet that's a *great* way to meet people."

I noticed that Martha put as much distance between herself and Karen as she could without being rude. Dawn managed to persuade Karen to stay with Claud and Andrew, then she and I took Jill and Martha to the swim team side of the pool.

We sat near the lifeguard stand and watched

the team go through their warm-up exercises. Dawn told Jill she used to be on a swim team in California and how much she liked it. Meanwhile, I talked to Martha about how much fun it was to swim. And she told me she took swimming lessons at the day camp she went to in Boston.

When the team was practicing the butterfly stroke, Jill proudly announced, "I can do that."

"Can Martha?" I asked.

"Sure, she's a good swimmer, too," Jill said. "Especially for a little kid. We both passed intermediate."

I winked at Dawn. She smiled back. Our idea just might work.

Two coaches were conducting the swim team session. I decided that the one with the whistle and clipboard was the head coach. "Is it too late for kids to sign up for the team?" I asked her.

"No. Anyone who's passed Beginners can join," she told me.

"I'm asking for two sisters who might like to join," I said. "One is ten, the other is seven."

"Have them come on over," she said.

I returned to Dawn and the girls. "If you've passed Beginners you can be on the team."

Jill leaped up. "All right!" she said. "Come on, Dawn. You and I can join."

"Jill, you know I'm going back to Stoneybrook next week," Dawn said. "I can't join. But you and Martha could. And I'd watch your practices every day until I leave."

Jill sat down again. "I'm not doing it if you aren't, Dawn," she said emphatically.

"Martha, you could join anyway," I said. "I know you like to swim."

"If Jill doesn't do it, I won't," Martha whispered to me.

Just then the instructor approached us. "You must be the new girls," she said to Martha and Jill. "We sure could use you on the team."

Jill said, "No, thanks."

Martha looked at the ground and didn't say anything.

"Martha and Jill are still thinking about it," Dawn told the coach.

"We're having a mini-fair tomorrow — a fundraiser, put together by the kids, with games and a bake sale," she said. "Why don't you all come? It'd be a great way to meet the other kids on the team and talk to them about it."

We said thanks and that we would be there.

"Hope to see you tomorrow, Martha and Jill," the coach said as she headed back to her team.

Just then I noticed Karen making her way toward us. The last thing Martha needed now was Karen's over-exuberant efforts.

"Let's go back to the other side of the pool and do some swimming," I said. While Dawn took the girls in the water, I sat by the kiddie pool where Claudia was watching Andrew, and told Claud about the mini-fair.

"That sounds like fun," Claud said. "I wonder what we could do to help? I know! Maybe they would let us have a face-painting booth."

When the swim team practice was over, Claud and I told the coach our idea. She thought it was terrific.

Then we told our kids.

"I want Claudia to make me a cat," Karen said. "What do you want to be, Martha?"

Martha said, "I don't know."

"I want to be a frog," Andrew said.

Karen asked Jill how she wanted her face painted.

"However Dawn has hers," Jill answered.

After swimming and fooling around at the pool, we were all pretty hungry. So we went to the harbor and bought lunch from an outdoor stand, then sat near the dock and watched the boats while we ate. Andrew was thrilled.

When we finished our lunch I told Dawn, "The historical society is open this afternoon. I'd like to go over there for a little while."

"The girls are pretty wiped from swimming," Dawn said. "And Andrew could use a nap. Claud and I can take them back to the house and you can go alone." I thought that was an excellent idea. I had some serious research to do, and it'd be easier to do it without baby-sitting responsibilities.

The historical society is in an old brick house off Main Street. The door was open, so I walked inside. It was dark and cool. After the bright light and heat of the outdoors, it felt wonderful.

A tiny white-haired woman was sitting at a small table in the front hall. "Good afternoon," she chirped. "May I help you?"

"I'm interested in learning more about the old houses around here," I told her. "This seems like a good place to start."

"Indeed it is," she said. She stood up. "I'm Eleanor Butterfield and I'll do what I can to assist you."

I explained that I was mostly interested in the Randolph mansion. "I'm hoping you have some old architectural plans of the house," I said.

She led me into the front parlor, which serves as the historical society library. "I believe we have something in the vertical files," she said. I followed her to a file cabinet.

While she was going through old documents, I told her that I'd heard about "A Historical Tour of Reese" by Millicent Ellsworth.

"Oh, yes," she said. "But Millicent got a bit carried away with her stories. She had a flair for the dramatic."

When I asked what she meant by that, Mrs. Butterfield explained, "Millicent's dates for births, deaths, fires, and such were all accurate. But when it came to personal stories, she was known to exaggerate and even veer from the truth."

I related the story of Reginald and Mary Randolph that Claudia had read in "A Historical Tour of Reese."

"Well, my dear," Mrs. Butterfield said, "some people like to believe those stories. I suppose it's good for tourism. The facts about Mary Randolph are these. She had two children and six or so grandchildren. Her son and his family lived at the mansion with her. It was a lively place back then. I've seen references in diaries and journals to parties and hunts and all sorts of joyous events at the mansion in the years that Mary was a widow. And I've seen her name listed among those who did volunteer work at the local hospital and for the Seamen's Widows and Orphans Society. I expect Mary Randolph did indeed grieve for her husband. Perhaps she even took to the widow's walk now and again. But she wasn't 'flung to her death' from it in a storm. Town records inform us she died in her sleep."

Mrs. Butterfield pulled a file from the cabinet and handed it to me. "Here we are," she said. "Architectural drawings of the Randolph mansion. You're not allowed to take this file from the room, but you may spend as much time as you like with it here."

Mrs. Butterfield returned to her desk in the hall. I sat at a table in the library and studied the original floor plans. Once I got used to the way they were drawn I looked for familiar things such as the kitchen, our bedrooms, and the staircase to the fourth floor. My objective was to see if there was anything in the drawings that I didn't recognize — such as a secret passage.

I noticed that what looked like a closet on the first floor drawing was labeled "dumbwaiter." It was there on the third-floor drawing, too. This one was in the "children's playroom." I studied the location of the children's playroom. It was Dawn's bedroom.

Mrs. Butterfield returned to the library to see how I was doing and to ask if I had any questions.

"I was wondering if you could tell me what a dumbwaiter is," I said.

"My, yes," she said. "It's a small elevator used to move food from one floor to another." She traced the plan with a forefinger. "In the

Randolph mansion it went from the kitchen to the children's playroom, where the nanny would serve the younger children their meals. As you can imagine, a dumbwaiter came in quite handy. You see, trays of food could be sent up, and dirty dishes sent down, without all that stair-climbing. Just with the pull of a rope."

"So there are doors that open to the dumbwaiter in each of those eating rooms?" I asked.

"That's correct," she said.

After I copied the parts of the drawing that I wanted to show my fellow detectives, I took the file to Mrs. Butterfield. "Thanks," I said. "You've been very helpful."

"You know what's curious?" she asked.

"What?"

"As you can see, we don't have many visitors here. But you're the second person this month who's asked for information about the Randolph mansion."

"Who was the other person?" I asked. (I figured it would be Mr. or Mrs. Menders, after they inherited the estate.)

"She didn't tell me her name," Mrs. Butterfield answered. "But I do remember that she spoke with a thick accent." An accent? Well, that definitely ruled out the Menderses.

I left the historical society feeling both pleased and puzzled.

Claudia

Wednesday
11 p.m.

I am so dispointed in Georgio. I hate that he acts like he's my freind (when all he wants is to steel.) I feel sory for his grandparrents.

By the way, remined me never to go to a scarey play when I'm in the midle of solving a mystery!

I was sitting in a lawn chair sketching the grove of pine trees.

"Hi!"

It was Georgio.

"Hi," I replied cautiously.

He sat on the grass next to me. "It looks like you have the afternoon off, too," he said.

"Everyone is having a quiet hour."

"How would you like go for a quiet walk with me?" he asked. He held up a bunch of herbs. "I'm taking my grandparents some herbs from their old kitchen garden."

"Your grandparents who were caretakers here?"

He nodded. "Do you want to come?"

"Sure." I closed my sketchpad. "I'll tell the others where I'm going. I'll be right back."

Even though Georgio gave me the creeps I knew I should go with him. I could ask his grandparents about the mansion, and work on finding the answer to what had become the biggest question of all for me: Is Georgio Trono the one who's trying to frighten us, and if so, why?

Despite my doubts about Georgio, I enjoyed our walk to his grandparents' apartment. Georgio loves his hometown, and I enjoyed hearing about what growing up in Reese was like for him. We passed his grammar school, and the firehouse where his father and grandfather served as volunteer firefighters. As we walked through the park where the Founders' Day celebration would be held, he asked me, "How's that float coming along?"

"We're thinking of a historical theme," I told him. "And wearing some of the old clothes we found in the attic."

"I don't think you should go up there."

"Why not?"

"I told you," he answered sternly. "No one's used that part of the house in years. I'm not sure it's safe. I'm sorry that I opened it up for you yesterday."

I'd spent all morning in that attic the day before, and I hadn't seen anything that looked dangerous. What was Georgio's *real* reason for not wanting us snooping around on the fourth floor?

Georgio announced that we'd reached his grandparents' house. The Tronos were pleased to see Georgio and to meet me. They served us homemade lemonade and fabulous brownies. And I didn't have to bring up the subject of the mansion . . . because *they* did.

"That's some big house, isn't it?" Mr. Trono said to me.

"It certainly is," I replied. "And beautiful. Do you miss it?"

"Oh, yes." Mrs. Trono passed me the plate of brownies. "But mostly we miss Mr. Randolph. He was a fine gentleman to work for, and, I daresay, a dear, dear friend. We took care of him to the very end."

"How did he die?" I asked.

"Oh, it was a long illness. He didn't know us toward the end. He was always mumbling on about the past, the way dying people sometimes do."

"About the past in the mansion?" I asked. This could be *very* interesting.

"He did mention the attic once or twice," Mr. Trono said.

Georgio interrupted. "Claudia isn't that interested in Mr. Randolph, Gramps. She wants to know how people dressed. Things like that. For a float she's doing for the parade."

Georgio was trying to change the subject because we were talking about the attic!

"I think the Menderses would be interested in knowing what their uncle was talking about on his deathbed," I said firmly. "And so am I."

"I suppose they would," Mrs. Trono said. "Mr. Randolph often said he wanted his 'treasure from the attic.' But nothing he said in

170

those last days made sense, so I've never believed there was any real treasure in the attic."

Treasure in the attic! That would explain a lot.

"I think you're right, Grandma," Georgio put in. "Those were just the mumblings of a dying man. There's nothing in the attic." (How did he know what was up there?)

I wanted to ask the Tronos about the dumbwaiter. But since I didn't want Georgio to suspect that I was doing detective work, I had to be careful how I brought up the subject. "What I like best about big old houses," I began, "are all the special features like verandas and butlers' pantries and dumbwaiters."

"Well, the mansion certainly has everything you've mentioned," Mr. Trono said.

"I haven't noticed a dumbwaiter," I said.

"Oh, the dumbwaiter has been covered up for years. We never used it. Mr. Randolph always liked to eat in the dining room off the veranda."

"And when he was sick we carried him his meals," Mrs. Trono added. She patted my hand kindly. "The dumbwaiter could be dangerous, dear, so do stay away from it."

Georgio stood up. "We have to go now," he said abruptly.

In a minute we were all standing at the front

door. "What a lovely visit," Mrs. Trono said. "Claudia, I do hope you'll come visit us again sometime."

I said thank you and goodbye, and we left. As I walked down the street with Georgio I thought over the evidence I'd gathered. I was more certain than ever that he was the "ghost" trying to scare us sitters and the kids. And now I knew why he was doing it. He wanted to find Mr. Randolph's treasure and keep it for himself.

Wednesday was our night off. We had big plans — pizza and the summer stock production of *Dracula*. I put on my black gauze skirt and a red tank top, and tied my white silk bomber jacket around my waist. Then I put on my airplane earrings. Dawn, Kristy, and Mary Anne came into my room to keep me company.

I told them everything that had happened at the Tronos', including the part about Georgio not wanting his grandparents to tell me anything.

"So our 'ghost' probably isn't a ghost," Mary Anne said.

Dawn wanted to review all the clues again, but it was time to leave.

I loved having the evening off. And — believe it or not — Lionel was part of the fun. On the way to town he made us laugh so hard we couldn't stop. He would speak in different accents and we'd try to guess where he was supposed to be from. I was the worst at guessing. When he put on a Scottish accent I thought it was Australian.

We took a big booth in the pizza parlor and ordered a pizza deluxe. While we were waiting for the pizza, we quizzed Lionel about his ghostly activities at the beginning of the week.

"Did you play hallway ghost two nights in a row?" Dawn asked.

"Yes," he confessed.

"What color candle did you carry the *first* night?" I asked.

"Orange. But after I saw you guys inspecting the carpet, I realized the wax had dripped. So I bought white candles — dripless ones. A ghost wouldn't drip wax, would it?"

"That's debatable," I answered.

"Lionel, where did you find the orange candle you used that first night?" Dawn asked.

"In the gardener's shed, where Georgio keeps his tools," he said matter-of-factly. "And speak of the devil . . ."

Lionel was looking toward the front door. Georgio had come in and spotted us. Or had he spotted us and then come in? In any case, he strode to our table and treated us like long lost friends.

After everyone had said hi, Georgio asked, "Mind if I join you?"

Naturally, we couldn't object. As we made room for Georgio, Lionel told him, "We were just talking about you."

"I hope you only said great things," Georgio replied. He was looking at me when he said that. I felt myself blush.

Mary Anne said, "We're going to see *Dracula* tonight." Mary Anne was trying to change the subject, but her effort boomeranged, because Georgio said, "I know some of the guys working on that production. Do you mind if I come with you?"

I wanted to say, "I *do* mind. Leave us alone!" But how could I do that? Especially when Georgio told us he'd be happy to introduce Lionel to his friends who were working on the play.

We spent the rest of our time at the pizza parlor making plans for our Founders' Day float. Georgio insisted that *he* should bring the clothes down from the attic for us, and he repeated what he had said to me at his grandparents', that the fourth floor wasn't safe.

I noticed Mary Anne's eyes growing round with fright and Kristy looking suspiciously at

Georgio. They were probably thinking what I was thinking. Get me away from this guy!

Going to the play was scary beyond words. I didn't know who to be more afraid of in that darkened theater — Count Dracula on the stage or Georgio off the stage (he was sitting next to me).

By the time we left for home Lionel was hyper-excited. Georgio had introduced him to the teenaged ushers at the theater. They seemed to like Lionel, and said if he came by before the performance the following night he could meet all the people involved in the production and help pass out programs. I was in a hyper state, too: hyper freaked-out by the dark, moonless night, Lionel's nonstop imitation of Count Dracula, and Georgio (who insisted on walking beside me all the way home).

When we reached the mansion, Lionel raced ahead. He probably couldn't wait to tell his folks about the theater group and the connections he had made. As the rest of us walked around to the back door, Georgio pointed to the fourth floor. "Look at that," he said. "You guys must have left a light on up there."

"Yeah," I said, "I guess so."

By then I think we all figured that somehow he was responsible for that light. So none of us would give him the satisfaction of seeming scared.

Then we all saw it — a flutter of white fabric moving across the widow's walk. Mary Anne let out a frightened squeak and Dawn gasped. Otherwise we remained calm. Or pretended we were calm. I wanted to scream and run all the way home to Stoneybrook.

Naturally, Georgio saw the figure in white too, but he acted surprised (the rat!). "Something weird is going on here," Georgio whispered to me. "I don't want to frighten anyone, but, Claudia, I want you to promise me you won't go to the fourth floor again."

"Sure," I said. "I promise." *I* knew what was weird. Georgio. I was so disappointed in him. I'd hoped he was a nice guy.

That night I slept in Dawn's room again. I heard the woman's scream in the wall that she'd told me about. I reminded myself, it's just Georgio's female accomplice, not a ghost. But it wasn't all that comforting. I couldn't help wondering what Georgio's next step might be. I was still lying awake, feeling upset, and frightened of more things than I could keep track of.

CHAPTER 16

ANDREW

DEAR DADDY,
RIBB-ID. I'M A FROG. I SAW A BOAT.
X X OO
ANDREW

I went to the mini-fair. Claudia painted faces.

Karen was a cat.

Martha was a mouse.

Jill was a teenager.

Guess what I was? Rib-id.

Claudia made lots of kids look like animals. She gave all the money to the swim team.

Martha made a new friend today. Karen didn't help her at all. Martha's friend is Jody. Jody is on the swim team. Jody wanted to be a mouse like Martha.

My baby-sitters are silly. At the fair they followed ladies who talked like Mary Poppins. Kristy said, "Andrew, I'm looking for someone, but I don't want her to know. It's a secret."

Some of the people we followed were baby-sitters. Mary Poppins was a baby-sitter, too. But some of the other ladies were on vacation.

I asked Mary Anne, "How come people talk funny on vacation?" She said people come to America with their "accents." When I go on a trip I take a suitcase.

Claudia asked one lady, "Do you know the way to Randolph Mansion?"

A silly-billy question! Claudia knows how to get to the mansion. We all know the way back. The lady thought it was a silly-billy question, too. She said, "No. Should I?"

Claudia told Kristy, "I give up."

CHAPTER 17

Dawn

Thursday
5:00 p.m.

I think we did a better job today at helping the Menders kids. Martha made a friend at the fair, and Jill spent an afternoon without me (a major accomplishment!). The biggest surprise of all is that Lionel and Jason have a common interest. If we could just persuade Jill and Martha to join the swim team, I think all four Menders kids would be happy — at least for the rest of the summer.

Now our biggest (and toughest) job is to identify the villains (or ghosts?) in the Menderses' new home. By the time we leave Reese, this mystery must be solved.

I learned something about myself today. I hate being trapped in small, dark spaces!

"Dawn, do I have to go to the mini-fair if I don't want to?" Jason asked me.

Except for Jason, all the kids were excited about going to the fair, particularly because we were setting up a face-painting booth. When I told Kristy what Jason had said, we agreed that Jason shouldn't be forced to go, and that I'd stay with him. I had a theory that Jill might have a better chance of making new friends at the mini-fair if I wasn't there. Kristy agreed, adding, "I also want Jason to get used to going to the playground without me."

After the others had left for the fair, I turned to Jason and said, "Let's go to the ballfield and you can play softball."

"Not without Kristy," he said.

"Kristy's going home in a few days," I reminded him. "What will you do then?"

Jason shrugged his shoulders.

"Okay, well, how about playing catch here for a little while?" I suggested. I figured after we threw a ball around, I'd bring up the idea of going to the playground again.

We tossed the ball back and forth. I could tell that Jason was a little bored playing with me (softball is *not* my sport). So when I saw Lionel, I tossed the ball to him. The ball didn't go where Lionel could easily reach it, but still he caught it. I was surprised — and impressed.

Lionel threw the ball to Jason, and Jason tossed it back to him. "Lionel," I called out, "I have to go inside for a minute. Would you play with Jason until I come back?"

"I think I'm doing that," he said.

The brothers were playing together for the first time that week. Inside I made fresh lemonade. When I went back out with it, Lionel was showing Jason how to throw a knuckleball.

While they were guzzling down the lemonade, I said, "Lionel, you seem to know a lot about softball."

"His team won the Massachusetts Little League championship," Jason said proudly. "He has a big trophy."

"That's great, Lionel!" I exclaimed. "So why

don't *you* take Jason to the ballfield?"

Jason's eyes grew wide with excitement. "Would you?" he asked his brother.

"I suppose I could," Lionel answered. "But I'm not a jock kind of guy anymore. I'm an actor."

"Think of it as a part in a play," I suggested, "and act the role of a guy who loves softball and is going to the ballfield with his kid brother."

"Hey," he said, "not a bad idea."

I noticed that Lionel was wearing white linen pants and a beige short-sleeved shirt. "And don't forget costuming," I suggested. "You might want to dress the part, too."

"Right again," he said. "Be back in five."

A few minutes later Lionel appeared before us in cutoff jeans, a T-shirt that read "Boston Red Sox," and a baseball cap turned sideways. "It's all in the details," he told me.

After they took off, I was alone at the mansion. At first I thought I'd go to the mini-fair and catch up with the others. Then I decided this was a perfect opportunity to work on our mystery. I lay in the hammock reading over our vacation notebook, reviewing clues, and doing some strategic planning. By the time I figured out what our next step should be, Lionel and Jason had returned.

Dawn

I met them on the lawn halfway between the hammock and the house. They each carried a quart bottle of Gatorade. Jason was grinning from ear to ear. "Lionel's going to be our coach!" he announced.

"Lionel," I exclaimed, "that's wonderful! It's absolutely fabulous."

"Now we have the best coach of any team." Jason said.

Lionel gulped from his bottle. "It's a long role," he told me, wiping his mouth with the back of his hand. "But I can handle it." He gave his brother a friendly punch on the arm. "Way to go, right, buddy?"

When Jason went running off to the kitchen for a snack, Lionel told me, "This'll work out great. Playing softball will help keep me in shape, which is very important in acting. And I'll still be free at night to work at the theater." I had a feeling Lionel wasn't going to be bored in Reese after all.

During the next half hour everyone returned home and congregated on the veranda. We admired Claud's face paintings. Then, Lionel, who'd showered and changed back into his white linen trousers, left for the theater. The parents took the rest of the kids for a late afternoon walk along the beach. The Coopers were out buying groceries. So the four baby-sitters were finally alone at the mansion.

I asked Kristy if they'd identified the woman with the accent at the mini-fair. I knew they'd planned to do a little sleuthing while they were there.

"*The* woman?!" Kristy exclaimed. "We found a *dozen* women with accents." She explained that some of the wealthy people who summer in Reese have European nannies, who speak English with an accent.

"And a tour group of women from England were at the fair," Claud added. "They all have heavy British accents."

"And don't forget the two French families who are here for the summer," Mary Anne said.

"The result of the BSC Mini-Fair Spy Operation," Kristy concluded, "was that we looked pretty foolish. Even Andrew noticed."

"Well, I have a plan," I said. "Since everyone is gone, this is the perfect opportunity to check out that dumbwaiter. I think it's an important clue."

We went to the kitchen together. Mary Anne looked around the room. "The dumbwaiter should be next to the pantry," she whispered. "I bet it's behind that painting."

Dawn

It took two of us to lift the big painting off the wall. And sure enough, under the painting was a pair of wooden doors.

"Who's going to open them?" Mary Anne asked nervously.

"I'll do it," I volunteered. I put my hands on the metal handles.

"Mary Anne and I will stand guard and warn you if anyone is coming," Kristy said. She stood near the door that led from the kitchen to the outside. Mary Anne watched at the door to the dining room in case someone came in through the veranda.

"Be careful," Mary Anne told me. "Don't do anything dangerous."

"Here goes," I whispered to Claud as I slowly turned the handles and pulled the doors open.

We faced a large opening, with pulley ropes to our right and left. We leaned inside and looked up. "The shelves must be up there someplace," Claud said. "Let's pull."

As I pulled on the rope we heard an awful squeaking noise. "That's one of the noises I've been hearing in my wall," I told Claud. Looking up, I could see the bottom of the dumbwaiter coming down toward us. "Whoever is trying to scare us has been pulling the dumbwaiter up and down to make that noise . . ."

Suddenly Claud screamed, "Watch out!"

Instinctively I ducked. Something jumped out of the dumbwaiter and sailed over my head.

"It's okay, Dawn," Claud said. "It was the cat."

Kristy jumped out of Spooky's way as he streaked by her and flew out of the kitchen. "How did he get in there?" she asked.

I pulled the rope to send the dumbwaiter up again. "I heard something fall down here when Spooky jumped out," I told Claud. We leaned into the space and looked down to the bottom of the shaft.

"I see something," Claud said. I saw it, too. It was the size of a paperback book, but that's all I could tell in the darkness. "It might be important," I told Claud. "I'm going to go in there and get it."

"No," Mary Anne said. "Dawn, don't." She wanted to grab me away from the dumb-waiter, but she wouldn't leave her post. "Please," she pleaded in a hoarse whisper.

"It's so dark down there," Claud said. "And what if someone comes?" She sounded as frightened as I was feeling.

I knew if I thought about it any longer I wouldn't do it, so I climbed in and dropped about four feet down to the floor of the shaft.

Above me I could see the bottom of the dumbwaiter shelves, and Claud peering anxiously
down at me. The place gave me the creeps. I
wished I had listened to Mary Anne. I couldn't
wait to get out of there.

I bent over and picked up the object I'd seen.
"It's a tape recorder," I called up to Claud.

"We should put it back in the dumbwaiter,"
she said. "We don't want to leave any evidence that we've been here."

I was feeling more claustrophobic by the
second. "Hand me a chair," I told Claud, "so
I can climb out."

Just then I heard Kristy hiss, "You guys, the
Coopers are coming."

Claud's face registered total panic. And I
was *terrified* of being closed in that damp, dark
hole but I still told Claud, "Shut the doors."

Claud whispered, "We'll come back as soon
as we can," and closed me in.

I was in total darkness.

I heard the scraping noise of the painting
being replaced on its hook. The next things I
heard were footsteps above me and Elton
Cooper cheerfully greeting my friends: "Good
afternoon, girls. What are you all doing in-
doors on such a pretty day? . . . Oh, you aren't
all here. One of you is missing."

"Dawn went to town," Kristy said quickly.

"Funny, we didn't pass her on the road," Elton said. My heartbeat was pounding in my ears.

"She caught a ride," Claudia put in.

"And we're getting a snack," Kristy said. I heard the refrigerator door close. "Snacks for the hungry baby-sitters."

"Can we help you with anything?" Mary Anne asked. I could hear the tremor in her voice. Could Mr. Cooper?

"You could bring the rest of the grocery bags from the back of the car," he said.

I heard my friends hurry outside.

Oh, no. They were leaving me alone with the Coopers! What if the Coopers didn't leave the kitchen until after dinner? What if I had to stay in this dark, hot hole for hours and hours? What if I ran out of oxygen and fainted — or worse. If they opened the dumbwaiter and found me, what would they do?

"Did you remember to buy the sausage for the meatballs?" I heard Elton ask.

A woman's voice answered, "You told me to, didn't you?"

"You shush, Maggie," Mr. Cooper scolded. "Those girls will be right back."

I thought, Maggie is a nickname for Margaret. The hair rose on the back of my neck.

A minute later I heard the thumps of grocery

bags being set on counters and Kristy saying, "Mr. and Mrs. Cooper, you've been cooking us such great meals and everything. We want to do something for you for a change. So Mary Anne is going to serve you afternoon tea on the veranda while Claudia and I put the groceries away."

Please, I prayed. Please say yes.

Elton protested that it was their job to serve us tea. I held my breath. But finally he said, "Well, I was just thinking that Margaret could use a break."

"And you'll take the break with her," Kristy insisted.

"Thank you," Elton said. "I will."

Thank you, Kristy. Thank you.

I heard the departing footsteps of the Coopers, then the sound of the painting being taken down. Finally the doors of the dumbwaiter opened and I could see Claud's face above me. She handed me a chair. "Hurry," she whispered. I stood on the chair and climbed out of my prison. Claud leaned over and pulled up the chair. We quickly drew the shelves down and replaced the tape recorder on the middle shelf. "I bet if we played the tape we'd hear a woman's scream," Claud said.

When we'd raised the shelves again, we

latched the dumbwaiter closed and put the painting back. Meanwhile, Mary Anne was practically having a heart attack, while Kristy made tea for the Coopers.

"Dawn, you better get out of here," Mary Anne whispered. "In case they come back."

Before I left the kitchen I told my fellow BSC detectives the most important thing I learned in the bottom of the dumbwaiter shaft: "You guys," I whispered, "Mrs. Cooper can talk."

CHAPTER 18

Mary Anne

Thursday
7:30 p.m.

I don't have any ghosts on my suspects list. Just four LIVE suspects.

Suspect #1: The woman with the European accent.

Evidence: Making inquiries about the Randolph mansion at the historical society.

Suspects #2 & #3: Margaret and Elton Cooper.

Evidence: Telling us and the kids scary stories. Lying to the Menderses. Pretending Mrs. Cooper can't speak.

Mary Anne

Suspect #4: Georgio Irono.

Evidence: Has key to fourth floor and doesn't want us going up there. Thinks there's treasure in the attic.

If Georgio is our criminal, are the Coopers his partners in crime? Or is the woman with the accent his female accomplice? Or is Georgio the Coopers' accomplice?

"Thank you so much, Mary Anne," said Mr. Cooper. "Doesn't that tea tray look splendid."

I was walking across the veranda with a tray of tea, pound cake, and sliced peaches.

"Mrs. Cooper thanks you, too," Mr. Cooper added. When Mrs. Cooper flashed me a smile it gave me the creeps. I thought, she could thank me herself. She can speak.

"You're welcome," I said. I could hear my voice shaking. I placed the tray on the wicker coffee table in front of the Coopers.

Back in the kitchen, I told Claudia, "I think it's time to ask the Tronos some more questions." She agreed, and called them to see if it was okay if she dropped by for a visit and brought a friend. Dinner was scheduled for eight o'clock. If we hurried, we could spend half an hour with the Tronos and be back before we were missed. Kristy and Dawn said they'd stay behind to keep an eye on the Coopers.

"Be careful," I warned them.

"You, too," Kristy said.

I reminded her that the Tronos weren't suspects.

"But their grandson is," Dawn replied. I saw Claudia frown. She had been spending a lot of time with Georgio.

"We'll be careful," I told Kristy and Dawn.

As we hurried through the streets, I asked Claudia, "What if Georgio's at his grandparents'?"

"He went into New Hampshire to buy some special paint for the float. He won't be back for ages."

The Tronos were just as sweet and nice as Claudia had described them. We talked about Founders' Day and enjoyed a glass of iced tea before we peppered them with questions.

I began with, "Do you know the Coopers very well?"

Mrs. Trono looked at me quizzically and asked, "The Coopers?"

"Margaret and Elton Cooper," Claudia said. "The new caretakers at the Randolph estate."

"We met them once," Mrs. Trono replied, "when we gave them our keys. Poor Mrs. Cooper can't talk. I remember that."

"I always think of everybody knowing each other in a small town like Reese," I commented.

"But the Coopers aren't from Reese, dear," Mrs. Trono said. "I've lived in Reese all my life. I would have known them if they were."

So the Coopers had lied to the Menderses about where they were from. I didn't want to alarm the Tronos, so I changed the subject.

"Was there a key to the fourth floor staircase in the set of keys you gave to the Coopers?" I asked.

"Certainly," Mr. Trono answered. "I gave them a complete set. On my own keyring."

"I suppose a key could have fallen off," Claud suggested.

"Not from that keyring," Mrs. Trono said. "It's a fine old thing. When you're a caretaker,

195

your set of keys must be secure on their ring. You live by your keys."

"Georgio asked about our key to the fourth floor, too," Mrs. Trono said. "Is everything all right at the mansion?"

I didn't want to worry these nice people. They'd have enough to worry about if Georgio were our culprit. So I said, "We've been doing some research on the mansion. About its history and everything."

"Like the story about Lydia Randolph," Claud added. She asked the Tronos if they'd heard the tragic tale of Lydia Randolph and George.

"Well," Mr. Trono said when Claudia had finished the story, "I've never heard such an outlandish bit of nonsense in all my life. That sounds like the kind of silliness Millicent Ellsworth would come up with. It's probably in that book of hers."

Mrs. Trono added, "You girls should know that the Randolph family have been outstanding citizens and benefactors of this town since its founding two hundred and fifty years ago. They loved their children and would want nothing but their happiness. They would never imprison their own daughter."

We left soon after that. As we were walking

up the gravel driveway to the mansion, Claud asked me, "Do you think Georgio is trying to help us or scare us?"

"I think maybe he's been trying to help us," I said. Claudia smiled at that. "I think it's just the Coopers we have to be afraid of," I added. "I don't trust them one bit."

"Me, either," Claud said. "But I'm not afraid of Georgio anymore. My gut feeling is that he's a good person. I really don't believe he'd want to do anything to frighten me — I mean us."

By then we'd reached the mansion. I went upstairs to clean up for dinner and to write in our vacation notebook. Later, downstairs, I found dinner laid out buffet-style on the veranda. The children were happy but tired after the mini-fair and the beach outing with their parents. When we'd all sat down to eat, Mr. Menders tapped his glass with a spoon and asked for our attention. He said if it was all right with the sitters, the adults would go to Boston the next day.

"But we'll be back tomorrow night," Mrs. Menders added. "And we'll all spend Founders' Day together."

Mr. Menders continued, "Our plan for the trip to Boston is to check out some wholesale sources for health foods." He looked at each of his children as he spoke their names. "Lionel. Jill. Jason. Martha. You should know that your mother and I are thinking very seriously of a permanent move to Reese. But, as I promised, I want to hear what each of you thinks about living here. So speak up."

Lionel spoke up first. "I like it here better than I did at first."

"Me, too," Jason said.

"How about you, Martha?" Mrs. Menders asked.

Martha answered by asking, "Can Jody come for a sleepover some time?" Mr. and Mrs. Menders exchanged a smile. Martha was doing just fine.

"Can Dawn and her whole family come live with us?" Jill asked. "We have lots of room."

I pretended to cough into my napkin so Jill wouldn't see me laughing. I noticed that Kristy was doing the same thing.

"Well, I guess it's just about settled then. We'll ask our lawyer to notify my cousin about our decision."

"I didn't know you *had* a cousin," Jason said. "How come we've never met him?"

"I haven't seen Charles Randolph myself since we were both about four years old," Mr.

Menders explained. "I remember my uncle saying years later that Charles had moved to Europe. Scotland, I think."

"Why do you have to let this cousin know whether we decide to live here?" Lionel asked.

"Because the will stipulates that I inherit this mansion only if we live here full-time," Mr. Menders answered. "Otherwise it goes to my cousin Charles."

"Dad, why didn't you tell us this before?" Lionel asked. "It's a pretty important detail."

I wondered the same thing.

"We didn't want to put that extra pressure on you," Mrs. Menders explained. "This is a hard decision to make to begin with. We wanted to give you every advantage in adjusting to life here. If you were miserable we would turn down the offer of the estate and go on with our lives as they were. But as we see it, you're beginning to adjust very nicely."

All of the Menders kids admitted they liked Reese and living in the mansion, even Jill. I was glad — but I was also more than a little nervous about it.

Dawn whispered to me, "I just remembered. Margaret Cooper spoke with an accent."

"From what country?" I whispered back.

Dawn answered by shrugging her shoulders.

After dinner, Lionel said he was going to the theater, and asked if any of us wanted to go with him. We all said no. (He was doing great on his own, and we had some sleuthing to do.) But I had an idea. "We'll walk you to the gate," I said, "if you'll play the accent game with us again."

I was hoping Dawn would recognize what country Mrs. Cooper's accent was from by listening to Lionel's repertoire of accents.

"Only this time," I told Lionel as we escorted him down the drive, "let's see if you can say the same short sentence with each of the accents. That'll make it harder for you and for us. Okay?"

"Sure," he said. "I can do that."

Dawn had caught on. She told him to use the sentence, "You told me to, didn't you?"

Lionel began. We identified a French accent and a Swedish accent. Both times Dawn shook her head no, meaning that wasn't the way Mrs. Cooper had spoken.

Then Lionel said, "Ye told me toe, didn't ye?"

Dawn asked him to say it again.

He did.

Dawn whispered, "That's it."

"So what country is it?" Lionel asked.

"Scotland — it's Scottish," Kristy said.

Lionel said she was right.

I felt a chill course through my body. Looking around at my friends, I could tell we were all thinking the same thing. If Mrs. Cooper had a Scottish accent, then . . .

We said a quick good-bye to Lionel and raced back to the house. We practically ran up the stairs, and straight to my room. As soon as the door was closed, Dawn blurted out, "Elton Cooper must be Tom Menders' cousin!"

"And Margaret is his *Scottish* wife," I added.

"And they're trying to scare us — and the kids — because they want the mansion for themselves," Claud concluded.

"But we still have to prove it, you guys," Kristy said. "We need more evidence."

We decided that the next day we'd gather as much evidence as we could to prove our suspicions that Mr. "Cooper" was really Charles Randolph. Then, when the Menderses returned from Boston we would tell them the whole story.

That night I slept in Kristy's room again. When we heard footsteps on the top floor I was *more* frightened than I had been when I'd thought ghosts might be up there. Ghosts would be easier to deal with, I thought, than the deceitful Coopers. They wanted the mansion badly enough to come to America, impersonate caretakers, and do all the things they'd done to scare us and the kids. What else would they do? I wasn't sure I wanted to find out.

CHAPTER 19

Jessi

Today we found out why so few clients have been calling. I hope you guys aren't too disappointed when you come home and find there aren't a lot of baby-sitting jobs.

Jessi

"What if we don't have any messages today, either?" Mal asked. We were on our way to the Kishis' for our Friday BSC meeting.

I checked the machine the second we walked into Claud's room. No messages. I threw myself across the bed and moaned. "Mal, you know what this means, don't you? It means that we've ruined the reputation of the club. First the answering machine wasn't on for twenty-four whole hours, and then we had to turn down jobs."

"Claud and the others are having a ball — no problems, no worries," Mal said. "Meanwhile, we've destroyed the club."

"When clients call today," I said, "let's apologize about the answering machine and be sure to tell them when the others will be back. And also tell them that if they've been disappointed by the club over the last week, it's our fault."

"That's a great idea," Mal said, "except for one thing."

"What?"

"You may have noticed that the phone isn't exactly ringing off the hook. No one is calling. They probably figure it's hopeless. That there aren't any sitters."

"Then maybe we should call them and explain everything," I suggested.

"Okay," Mal agreed. "Who should we call first?"

"The clients we know the best," I said. "I'll start by calling the Braddocks."

My stomach was doing cartwheels as I punched in the telephone number for the Braddocks. Mrs. Braddock answered. "Hi, Mrs. Braddock," I said. "This is Jessi Ramsey."

Mrs. Braddock asked me how I was. I said fine and asked her how *she* was.

"I'm just running out the door," she said. "Everyone is packed in the van. We're going on a two-week camping trip."

"Have a wonderful time," I told her.

"What was it you wanted, Jessi?"

"Oh, nothing, really," I said. "Just letting you know that the Baby-sitters Club will be here for you when you come back. Call any time. You can always leave a message on the BSC machine. 'Bye."

I hung up the phone and told Mal, "The Braddocks haven't called because they don't need sitters. They're going on vacation." I handed her the phone. "I'll make a note about their schedule in the record book while you make the next call."

Jessi

She punched in the Perkinses' phone number, listened for a little while and hung up without speaking. "A machine answered," she explained. "It said, 'You've reached the Perkins residence. We're on vacation until July thirtieth. Messages for Bill Murphy can be left with this machine.' Since I didn't have a message for Bill Murphy," Mal continued, "I hung up."

"So the Braddocks and Perkinses haven't called for sitters because they're going on vacation," I said. "That's a relief." I was relieved enough to notice that I was hungry. "Let's find something to eat before we make any more calls."

We found a bag of Chuckle Rings under Claud's bed. Mal ripped them open and we dug in. Two green and one red Chuckle later I called the Arnolds and learned that Marilyn and Carolyn had gone to visit their grandmother for a week.

"We'll be calling for sitters as soon as they're back," Mrs. Arnold told me. "Hope you're all having a wonderful vacation."

Next Mal called the Addisons. When she hung up she told me, "Corrie and Sean are at sleepaway camp."

"This is great," I said. "People aren't calling because they don't need sitters, not because they don't want the BSC anymore. It makes sense."

"It does," Mal said as she stuffed a circle of green Chuckle into her mouth. I couldn't understand what she said next because of the way the candy stuck to her teeth.

"What did you say?" I asked.

She chewed and swallowed. "I said, 'I'm still hungry.' "

We both thought that was hilarious. We searched Claud's room for a snack that was a little more nourishing than candy, and we couldn't stop giggling.

Finally, we found a bag of blue corn chips. While we ate, we talked about how much fun the Reese contingent must be having and how we wished *we* were hanging around in a seaside town without a care in the world.

"The only fun thing happening here," I said, "is Celebrate America! Day, and we have to work then."

"And work hard," Mal added. "Do you realize that between us we'll be taking care of fifteen kids?"

"Maybe we should join forces and do some kind of activity with all of them," I suggested.

"But they're different ages, Jessi. What kind of activity can we do with kids ranging in age from two to ten?" Mal asked.

Jessi

"What do two-year-olds and ten-year-olds have in common?" I replied.

"Absolutely nothing."

"Kristy wouldn't let that hold her back," I said. "And neither would the others. They love challenges."

"You're right." I took the last red Chuckle out of the bag.

"Then let's come up with something wonderful to do with all the kids," she said.

I rolled the Chuckle Ring across the BSC notebook to Mal. "If someone invented the wheel," I said, "then we can figure out what to do with fifteen kids."

"Inventing the wheel might have been easier," Mal commented as she rolled the Chuckle back to me. I didn't know then that the idea we were looking for was in that round Chuckle.

CHAPTER 20

Kristy

Friday
9:00 p.m.

I am writing this by candlelight.
A terrible thunderstorm is raging.
The electricity and phones are out.
We're alone with six children — and
two evil adults. Above all else, we
must protect the children.

Kristy

"Kristy, having all you sitters here this week is working out even better than I'd hoped," Lisa said. "You're doing a terrific job."

It was just after breakfast on Friday, and the adults were getting ready to leave for Boston. I wondered if I should tell Lisa about the Coopers. I decided against it. We needed more proof. It would be incredibly embarrassing if we accused the Coopers, only to find out we'd been wrong. Besides, what were we accusing them of? Telling us scary stories? Making noises in the wall? Saying someone was mute when she wasn't? Being Scottish? We needed more evidence.

But first, I reminded myself, we had baby-sitting responsibilities. Dawn and I had cooked up an idea for persuading Jill to join the swim team. After the adults left for Boston we took her aside.

"Kristy and I have been talking about you, Jill," Dawn began. "Now that it looks like you'll be moving to Reese, we thought you might like to start a baby-sitting club of your own."

Jill's eyes widened with interest.

"We can explain how we run our club and answer all your questions about baby-sitting," I added.

"I have a question already," Jill said. "How did you learn how to baby-sit?" I held back a grin. Jill had asked the perfect question.

"By sitting for our own sisters and brothers," Dawn answered. "You know — the way Kristy sits for Karen and Andrew."

"Lionel is too big for me to baby-sit for," Jill said. "And Jason wouldn't let me."

"What about Martha?" I asked.

"She'd say I was treating her like a baby."

"You could baby-sit for Martha without telling her," Dawn explained. "Sometimes I do that with my brother, Jeff. When we're doing water sports, like sailing, I watch out for him. I've worked in a lot of baby-sitting practice that way."

"Hey, I know! If you and Jill were both on the swim team," I suggested, "you could watch Martha and have fun, too."

"Dawn has fun with me," Jill said happily. "And I'm younger than her."

"That's right," Dawn replied. "Now you understand an important idea about baby-sitting. You can have *fun* with the kids you sit for, even when they're your own brothers or sisters."

Just then Martha came out to the veranda for our what-are-we-going-to-do-today meeting and asked, "Dawn, what are we going to do today?"

"Martha, how'd you like to join the swim team?" Jill asked.

"I'm not joining unless you do," Martha muttered.

"But I'm going to," Jill told her. "We're both going to."

Martha smiled widely. "Goody," she said. "Goody, goody, and triple goody."

After our meeting, Lionel and Jason headed for the ballfield, saying they'd catch up with us at dinnertime. Claudia was spending the morning working on our Founders Day float. Dawn was taking the Menders sisters to the pool. Mary Anne and I headed into town with Andrew and Karen.

Our first stop was the photocopy shop. Claud had asked us to make four copies of a picture from one of the old Randolph family albums. It was the photo of the man who had looked so mysteriously familiar to her. After we left the copy shop, Mary Anne took us to the historical society. The door was open, so we walked in.

"Hi, Mrs. Butterfield," Mary Anne said to the woman at the front desk. While I distracted Karen and Andrew with a painting of a boat in a storm, I strained to hear Mary Anne's conversation with Mrs. Butterfield.

"I dropped by to ask you a question about the woman you told me wanted to know about the Randolph estate," Mary Anne was saying. "You said she had a heavy accent. Do you remember if it was a Scottish accent?"

"Yes, it could have been Scottish," Mrs. Butterfield replied. "But why don't you ask her yourself? She's here now." She pointed to the library. We looked in that direction. But no one was there. "She must have gone out the back way," Mrs. Butterfield explained.

I ran through the library to the side window. Sure enough, Margaret Cooper was hurrying down the street. Mrs. Butterfield appeared beside me. "There she is," she said. "It's too bad she left without meeting you. She was *so* interested in knowing who else was making inquiries about the Randolph Mansion." Ah-ha! So Margaret knew about us now. I was afraid of what she would do next.

When we were outside again Mary Anne and I decided that we should go back to the estate right away. We needed to warn Claud that Margaret knew Mary Anne had been doing research on the Randolph estate. And that we knew she could speak! I promised Karen and Andrew that when we returned to the mansion they could watch a video. So far we'd been able to steer the kids out of the scary situation and I intended to keep it that way.

Later, while Mary Anne set the kids up with a video, I went out to the shed, where Claud was supposed to be working on the props for the float. She wasn't there. I looked in the gardens for Georgio. He wasn't there.

When I reported back to Mary Anne she said, "Maybe they're upstairs."

"Claud told me she might hunt for clothes in the attic this morning," I said. "Come on."

The door to the fourth-floor staircase was unlocked.

"What if Mr. Cooper is up there?" Mary Anne whispered.

A cold, clammy feeling washed over me. We crept silently up the stairs. The first thing I noticed on the fourth floor was that the attic door was closed. The second thing I noticed was that the door to Lydia's room was open.

I signaled Mary Anne to stay where she was while I investigated. The closer I inched to that open door the more frightened I became. What would I see? What if whoever was in there saw *me*? The image of a white-haired woman answering to the name of Lydia flashed through my mind.

I held my breath and snuck a peek into the

room. Two figures — male and female — were bending over a wicker basket.

I gasped.

And Claudia and Georgio screamed, which made me scream. But Mary Anne screamed the loudest of all.

When we had calmed down, Georgio locked the door to Lydia's room and the four of us went to my room to talk. Mary Anne and I sat on my bed. Georgio and Claudia sat on the window seat. "Georgio knows everything and he's totally innocent," Claudia told us. "He's been suspicious of the Coopers himself."

"Something's bothered me about those two from the beginning," Georgio explained. "Even before you came here. When I realized they were trying to scare you guys, and they claimed not to have a key to the fourth floor, I got really suspicious."

"What about the treasure in the attic?" Mary Anne said.

"I thought that somehow the Coopers had heard about what Mr. Randolph said when he was dying, and then took the caretakers' job to try to find this so-called treasure for themselves. Now I know they want the whole place."

"So you've been hanging around us because

you were suspicious of the Coopers?" I asked.

"That's the second reason," Georgio said. He smiled at Claud. "The first reason I've been hanging around you is because of Claudia."

Claud looked shyly at the floor before saying, "Anyway, Georgio has a key to the fourth-floor bedroom we've been calling Lydia's room. So we went up there. We'd just figured out how the light has been going off and on when Kristy scared us."

"Sorry about that," I said. "Tell us about the light."

"The lamp is hooked up to a timer," Georgio explained. "The kind people use to make robbers think someone is at home."

"In this case the robbers are using it," I commented.

"They hid the timer in an old sewing basket," Claud continued. "We left it there so they won't know that we're onto them."

"They might already know," Mary Anne said softly. "At least, Margaret might." She told Claud and Georgio about Mrs. Cooper and the historical society.

"By the way," Claud told us, "before the Coopers left this morning, Elton reminded me that it's their day off. He said he and Mrs. Cooper wouldn't be back until this evening."

216

"Good," I said. "That gives us plenty of time to hunt for more evidence."

"Let's check out their rooms," Claud suggested.

"Isn't that invasion of privacy?" I wondered out loud.

"Look at all the creepy things they've been doing to us," Claud reminded me.

I thought about the kids. I was convinced that the Coopers were a threat to their safety.

"How are we going to get in those rooms?" I asked.

"I have a master key that should fit the lock," Georgio said. "While you're up there I'll weed the back garden. That way I can warn you if I see them coming back here."

"How will you warn us?" I asked.

"Their bedroom window faces the back garden," Georgio said. "So look out every couple of minutes. I'll take off my hat if I see them."

We heard footsteps then, and stopped talking about the Coopers. Then we heard children's voices singing the theme song from *The Little Mermaid*. Karen and Martha bounced into the room. Martha, her hair still wet from swimming, announced, "I'm on the swim team. So's Jill."

We all congratulated Martha and promised to go to the girls' first swim meet on Monday.

After lunch, Mary Anne said she'd watch the girls and Andrew while the rest of us explored the Coopers' rooms. "You coming, Claud?" I asked.

"I have to do something else," Claud answered in a vague, distracted voice. I thought maybe she'd drift off and spend the afternoon mooning over Georgio. But Georgio wasn't the man she had on her mind. "Did you two photocopy that picture?" she asked.

When I gave her the copies, she said she'd be in the dining room if we needed her.

Dawn and I took the back stairs to the Coopers' private quarters. As I turned Georgio's key in the lock I told Dawn, "I hate sneaking around like this."

"I love it," Dawn confessed. "And they deserve it!"

The door opened into a sitting room. It had no windows. "Let's start in the bedroom," I suggested.

Dawn began her search with the clothes closet while I peered out the bedroom window. I looked down at the garden and saw Georgio, in a straw hat, weeding with a hoe.

"There isn't much in here," Dawn said. "It's as if they haven't even unpacked." Then in a trembling voice she added, "Kristy, look." I turned away from the window and saw that

Dawn was holding up a floor-length white satin gown. "It was in the back of the closet," she explained. "It must be the dress that's missing from the armoire in the attic."

"And I bet you anything that's the dress that the ghost of Mary Randolph wears on the widow's walk," I added.

"I saw a desk in the other room," Dawn said. "I'm going to search it." While I kept an eye on Georgio and his hat I noticed that the sky was darkening. It looked as though a big storm were headed our way.

"Kristy," Dawn called, "come here." I ran into the sitting room. Dawn was huddled over the desk. "You have to see this," she whispered. She pointed to a page in a notebook:

Ten-Step Plan for when company leaves:
1. poison ivy oil on inside of Lionel's and Mrs. Menders' clothes
2. get Georgio fired for fooling around with sitter
3. plumbing breakdown
4. disappearance of Jason's baseball glove (and any replacements)
5. small electrical fire in Martha's bedroom

Fire?! These are evil people, I thought. They'll hurt even children to get what they want.

"I guess they're waiting until we leave to get serious," Dawn said. "And that's only half the list. Steps six through ten aren't here."

"Well, this is all the evidence we need," I told Dawn. "It *proves* that the Coopers are up to no good."

"And that Georgio is innocent," Dawn added. I had to agree with her.

Just then I thought I heard a car on the drive. I ran to the other room and looked out the window. Georgio's hat was on the ground beside him. "Hurry," I called to Dawn. "They're back."

We shoved the list in the drawer where Dawn had found it, locked the door to the rooms, and ran down the stairs. Margaret came into the kitchen from outside a split second after we entered from the back stairs. Had she seen us coming from her rooms? She smiled at me but her eyes were cold and calculating.

We later learned that while we were investigating the Coopers' quarters, Claudia was coming up with another piece of evidence incriminating the Coopers. She had gone to the dining room to experiment with the photocopies we'd made for her. She wanted to figure out why the man in the photo seemed familiar to her. She'd thought that the man reminded her of a woman she knew. To check that idea Claud drew wavy shoulder-length hair on the photocopy. Then she added eyeshadow and lipstick. The resulting image didn't remind her of anyone she knew. Looking at the hair she'd drawn on this female version of Mr. Randolph's ancestor gave Claudia another idea.

She began with a fresh photocopy. This time she added a beard and mustache. It still wasn't what she was looking for, but she felt that she was coming closer. She pulled out another copy. This time she added a more delicate mustache and a smaller beard. When she finished, Elton Cooper was looking at her from the doctored photocopy.

At that moment a clap of thunder startled Claud. She was even more startled when the thunder was followed by a male voice announcing, "Big storm coming. Stay away from the windows." Claud looked up and gasped. Elton Cooper was standing in front of her. She clapped her hand over the image that looked

Kristy

so much like him and said, "Thank you, I will." Then she gathered up her papers and clutched them to her chest. "I'll check on the kids." Hurrying from the room, she wondered if he had seen what she was doing.

CHAPTER 21

Dawn

Friday
11 p.m.

I almost wish I still thought this house was haunted. It would probably be really spooky to be here in this fierce storm with the electricity out, wondering whether a restless spirit was roaming the halls. But it wouldn't be as bad as knowing that a pair of calculating criminals is in the house with us. I've never been so scared in my life.

Dawn

Everyone except me has fallen asleep. I can't help thinking about that dreadful story Elton told us. What will the Coopers do next to try to frighten us and the children? I'm going to stay awake for as long as I can and keep watch over everyone.

Will the morning ever come?

"Dawn, Dawn — where are you?"

Jill ran into the kitchen and threw her arms around me.

"What's wrong?" I asked. "What is it?"

"I'm scared," she said.

Another clap of thunder rattled the air. I felt Jill shudder. "It's only a storm," I told her. "You're safe inside with us. Come on, we'll find the others."

Within minutes, the late summer afternoon became so dark that we had to turn on the parlor lights. And because the storm was so violent and close, we unplugged the TV and VCR. Then we tried to start up a game of Junior Pictionary, but the kids were distracted by the crashes of thunder and bolts of lightning, and by the window-rattling winds and torrential rains.

"What about Lionel and Jason?" Martha asked. "They'll get wet."

"They will get *very* wet," Karen added. "Completely soaked."

"They'll be all right," I assured the girls. But I felt more worried than I let on. I hoped Lionel knew that they shouldn't walk home from the softball field during a lightning storm.

Finally, the girls and Andrew started paying attention to Pictionary. Kristy took Mary Anne and Claudia out to the hall to tell them what we'd found in the Coopers' rooms. A few minutes later Mary Anne and Kristy came back and Kristy whispered to me, "Claud has something to show you."

In the hall, Claud handed me a picture. I looked at it and asked, "Where'd you find this drawing of Elton? Is it from a *wanted* poster?" I was more afraid of Elton than ever. "Is he wanted by the FBI?"

Claud explained that what I was looking at wasn't Elton Cooper, but one of the Randolph ancestors. The evidence was mounting that Elton Cooper really was Charles Randolph, Mr. Menders' cousin.

"While you were with the kids just now,"

Claud told me, "we made three rules to follow till we can tell the Menderses about the Coopers. One, don't go anywhere alone in the mansion. Two, don't leave any of the children alone — even for an instant. Three, don't act suspicious of the Coopers. We don't want them to know how much we know about them.

I agreed to obey the rules, then asked, "What time did the Menderses say they'd be back?"

"After dinner," Claud reminded me.

"Maybe they'll come early," I said hopefully, "because of the storm."

A clap of thunder preceded a crackling flash of lightning. Then the lights went out. Claud and I rushed back into the parlor to help Kristy calm the kids down.

"It's dark," Andrew said. "Is it night, Kristy? Do I have to go to bed? I'm not tired."

While Kristy explained to Andrew that even though it was dark it wasn't night, Claud and I told the girls that we were going to have a great adventure. "We'll pretend this is long ago, before people had electricity," Mary Anne said.

"Just like the characters we're going to play on the float," I added.

"Goody!" Karen said. "Let's find some

flashlights and pretend they're candles."

Claud and I left Kristy and Mary Anne with the kids while we searched for flashlights. "I wish Lionel and Jason were back," I told Claud as we made our way down the darkened corridor. At that instant a zigzag of lightning illuminated the figure of Margaret Cooper. She was tiptoeing toward us, carrying an unlit flashlight. Claud and I were so startled we didn't say anything at first.

Margaret silently turned the flashlight on and handed it to us. In that dull yellow light it was hard to tell if she was smiling or sneering.

We thanked her and returned to the parlor to give the flashlight to Kristy. Then we made our way to the kitchen to put together a snack for the kids as best we could in the darkened house. We were fixing peanut butter and crackers when we heard a knock on the outside kitchen door. I was expecting Lionel and Jason, but it was Georgio. A powerful gust of wind came into the room with him.

"Is everyone okay?" he asked.

Georgio was dressed in yellow raingear and high, black rubber fireman's boots. As we talked he pulled out of his pockets three flashlights, a bundle of storm candles, and a transistor radio.

"Do you think the kids' parents will be able to drive home in this storm?" Claud asked.

"I had hoped they were already back," Georgio said. "I doubt they can drive from Boston in this weather," he told us. "The safest thing for them to do would be to stay in Boston until it's over."

Elton came into the kitchen while Georgio was telling us that the storm was going to last for several hours and could cause local flooding. "You're on high ground so there's no danger of flooding up here," Georgio explained. He added that as an auxiliary volunteer fireman, he'd be keeping an eye on flood levels and checking that the residents of Reese were safe.

We told Georgio that Lionel and Jason weren't home. "I'll go look for them," he said. "And I'll check on you and the kids again as soon as I can."

"You don't need to worry about them," Elton said. "They're safe with Margaret and me."

Ha, I thought.

Before Georgio left, he squeezed Claud's hand and gave her a quick kiss on the cheek. "Be careful, Claudia," he warned. Then he opened the door and went back out into the storm.

I wondered if Elton was thinking he could use that kiss as evidence that Georgio was "fooling around with a sitter."

For the next hour we kept the children busy with games and singing. We all felt a little better when Lionel and Jason returned. Georgio, true to his word, had gone to the playground to look for them, and found them in the rec barn with a few other kids. He had taken all the kids home, then gone out into the storm again to help more stranded people. Claud was very proud of him.

Kristy and Mary Anne made sure to tell the Coopers that since it was their day off, we could manage our own dinner. When the Coopers protested, saying this was an emergency, Kristy told them that making dinner by candlelight would be a fun, distracting activity for our charges. But the real reason we'd decided to make dinner ourselves was that we simply didn't trust the Coopers. What if they tried to poison us or something?

We tried to keep our spirits up while we put together a cold supper of salads and sandwiches. Lionel was a terrific sport and told the kids funny stories. Every once in awhile we'd turn on the transistor radio and listen to the emergency storm reports. Each report included a warning to stay at home and not to drive. I was pretty sure that the adults would not be home that night.

"I'm cold," Karen complained.

"Me, too," Jill added.

They were right. The temperature was dropping. Kristy and Mary Anne went off to find sweaters and sweatshirts for everyone while the rest of us cleaned up the kitchen.

While we were working, Margaret and Elton Cooper came into the kitchen from upstairs. "It's getting nippy," Elton said. "I'm going to make a fire in the parlor. You all come in there as soon as you've finished in here." Had he been listening in on our conversation? Had he been spying on us? And wasn't there something about fire on the list the Coopers had made?

Half an hour later we were warming ourselves in front of a wood fire in the big front parlor.

"Let's tell scary stories," Jason said.

I didn't think that was a very good idea, but Karen and the others did, and Mr. Cooper jumped at the opportunity.

"I know a true story," he said. "It's about the people who used to live in this house."

He then told the story of Reginald and Mary Randolph — the one we'd read in Millicent Ellsworth's so-called history of Reese. But he

230

added another episode that even Millicent wouldn't have had the nerve to invent.

"In 1879, twenty years after Reginald's boat sank," Elton said, "a fishing vessel from Reese named *First Catch* was out at sea when a sudden summer storm threatened the lives of all on board."

Elton told his story with dramatic touches worthy of Lionel, but this was the basic plot. As the boat, *First Catch*, was being dangerously tossed by the waves, another boat, apparently untroubled by the storm, appeared beside it. The second boat led *First Catch* and its crew safely to shore. But instead of seeking safe harbor itself, the beacon boat headed back to sea.

In a flash of lightning, the Captain of *First Catch* saw the name of the other boat painted on its side: *Mary*. The captain knew that *Mary* was the name of Reginald Randolph's vessel, the one that had sunk twenty years earlier. He realized that what he'd suspected during their miraculous rescue was true. He and his crew had been saved by a ghost ship with a ghost crew. In his last glimpse of the phantom ship, the captain of *First Catch* saw a woman standing beside the captain. The woman was dressed in white.

The next morning the captain of *First Catch*

learned that Mary Randolph had perished the night before, "hurled to her death by the violent winds of the storm," (as Elton put it), on the very night that the phantom ship saved the captain and his crew."

While Elton was telling the story, Margaret left the room. I wondered what mischief — or worse — she was up to. Would we soon hear screams and creaking noises? Would a ghostly vision in white pass by the open parlor door? Just as Elton finished, Margaret returned carrying a tray with cups of hot chocolate.

There was a hush in the room. The children seemed frightened by Elton's story. And the baby-sitters were afraid of the Coopers.

Karen broke the silence. "Oh, goody!" she exclaimed. "Hot chocolate. I love it."

Margaret smiled what I used to think of as her "pretty smile." Now I thought of it as her "fake smile." What if she'd put poison in that hot chocolate? I jumped up and took the tray from her. "I'll serve it," I offered. "And you sit down, Margaret. It's your day off, remember?"

Clever Claud understood what I was doing and why. She stood up, too. "I'll help," she said as she handed the first cup of hot chocolate to Margaret. "Could you tell us if it's cooled off enough for the children to drink?"

Margaret took a sip of the cocoa, smiled, and made the okay sign. Now that Margaret had had some, we served the others.

"What splendid baby-sitters you girls are," Elton said. "Worrying about the cocoa being too hot. You think of everything."

Was he on to us?

After the children had finished their cocoa we wished the Coopers good night, though I, for one, didn't mean it. Jill took my hand as we climbed the stairs. "Dawn, I'm scared," she whispered. I noticed that Jason was staying as close as possible to his big brother and each of the other kids was holding a sitter's hand. We had no trouble convincing the kids that it was the perfect night for a "sleepover party" in Kristy's and Mary Anne's rooms.

But before settling down for the night we all sat around in Kristy's room to talk. We wanted to make sure the children understood that the story Elton told them was make-believe. Lionel was a big help. He demonstrated how Elton had changed his voice and used pauses to make the story scarier.

"But I *saw* the lady in white," Jill whispered fearfully.

"When?" I asked.

"Last night. Spooky jumped on my bed and woke me up. I wanted him to sleep on my

233

bed, but he ran away. I tried to catch him. That's when I saw her. I thought it was Claudia or Mary Anne practicing for the parade. But the lady didn't turn around when I said your names."

I knew who "the lady in white" was, but I was determined not to tell the kids that the Coopers were trying to scare them. However, I didn't want them worrying about ghosts either. I didn't know what to say.

All the kids were listening to Jill. "Then the lady in white opened the door and went upstairs to the attic."

"Was it a ghost?" Karen asked.

"I think so," Jill said.

"I don't like ghosts," said Martha.

"It wasn't a ghost," Kristy said firmly. "It was Mrs. Cooper in her nightgown or something. Maybe she was checking on us."

"It wasn't a nightgown," Jill said. "It was a fancy dress, like the ones in the attic."

"I bet it was Mary Randolph's ghost," said Jason.

"I'm sure it was Mrs. Cooper, Jill," I said. "She must have a very fancy nightgown. Maybe even an antique one. There's nothing to be afraid of."

"Well, I'm scared anyway," Jill said. "I hate it here. I want to go back to Boston."

"Me, too," Martha said.

I looked around at my friends. How would we ever calm these kids' fears? How would we calm our own? I couldn't wait for morning to come.

CHAPTER 22

Our baby-sitting charges had a great time on Celebrate America! Day. They were all in the parade.

Claud, thanks for saying we could eat anything we could find in your room. We ate a bag of blue corn chips and a bag of Chuckle Rings.

"Jessi," I shouted into the phone a couple of hours after our Friday meeting, "I've had a great idea. I know what we can do with the kids we're sitting for on Celebrate America! Day." I realized that Jessi was probably holding the phone about three feet from her ear by then. I lowered my voice. "We can be the 'BSC on Wheels' and decorate the kids and their wheels in red, white, and blue. Those wheel-shaped Chuckles inspired me."

"You mean the kids will ride bikes?" Jessi asked.

"Not just bikes," I said. "Whatever they want that's on wheels. Skateboards, roller blades, Big Wheels, anything. And we'll make a sign."

Jessi loved my idea. We spent forever on the phone making plans. When we hung up we both had a lot of kids to talk to — fifteen to be exact.

I started with my brothers and sisters by making "BSC on Wheels" the subject of conversation at dinner.

Adam, Byron, and Jordan wanted to skateboard in the parade. Since you can't do much to decorate a skateboard they promised that first thing the next morning, which was Celebrate America! Day, they'd help Vanessa,

Nicky, Margo, and Claire decorate their bikes.

My dad said since he was going to the parade anyway, he'd be an extra sitter and help out, especially during the parade. Good old Dad.

After dinner I helped my brothers and sisters pick out red, white, and blue clothes. I lent Vanessa my favorite T-shirt, which is red and white striped, with blue stars around the neck and sleeves. Adam said he'd wear a red baseball cap, Byron could wear a white one, and Jordan, blue.

Next I called the Rodowskys. Mrs. Rodowsky thought it was a great idea for us to "roll" together in the parade. But I knew it was more important that the Rodowsky kids like the plan. So I asked to speak to each of them, starting with Jackie.

"Sure," Jackie the walking disaster said when he heard the idea. "I haven't had an accident in a long time. And my bike's not busted anymore." I decided to ask my dad to keep an extra close watch on Jackie, the *rolling* disaster.

Shea, who's nine, said he'd be in the parade if the triplets would. When he found out that they were going to be skateboarding, he was triple excited, because he skateboards, too. Archie, who's only four, didn't quite follow what I was talking about, but his mother understood and said he could ride his Big Wheels in the parade. She also said she'd help the boys decorate their wheels first thing in the morning and give us an extra hand during the day if we needed it.

Jessi, meanwhile, went to the Braddocks' house. She invited Becca to go along with her.

"Can we Rollerblade there?" Becca asked. "You can teach me on the way."

"I don't want to start by teaching you on the street," Jessi told her sister. "Besides, we have to be back home before it gets dark. We should bike to the Braddocks' and back."

Becca is good friends with Haley Braddock, so she went with Jessi, even though she was angry about not being able to Rollerblade. And she pouted the whole way.

Seven-year-old Matt Braddock is deaf, which is why Jessi didn't just call the Braddocks on the phone. She could have called and talked to Haley and Mrs. Braddock, but she wanted to discuss "BSC on Wheels" with Matt, too. Matt communicates with American Sign Language (ASL), and Jessi's good at signing. (The rest of us sitters have learned some ASL too, but Jessi's the best.) When she signed to Matt about our idea for the parade, he signed back: "Good idea. I'll Rollerblade. I can wear blue jean shorts and a white shirt with a red sweatband around my head. Is that okay?"

Jessi signed, "It's better than okay. It's perfect!"

Haley liked the idea, too. She said (so Becca could understand) and signed (for her brother), "I think being in the parade will be a lot of fun, too. I'll ride on my skateboard and wear red tights and a big white T-shirt with a blue sash."

Biking home, Jessi was pleased with how well her visit to the Braddocks had gone. But she wasn't pleased with Becca, who continued to complain about not being able to Rollerblade in the parade.

"You can ride your bike," Jessi said.

"Haley's not riding her bike," Becca shot back. "She's skateboarding."

Jessi reminded Becca that Vanessa Pike would be on a bike. But Becca wasn't listening (or was pretending not to listen). She pulled ahead on her bike and stayed about a half a block ahead of Jessi all the way home.

Back at home, Jessi didn't even have time to talk to Becca, much less give her a Roller-blading lesson. She had to call the Mar-shalls. They were going to be Jessi's biggest baby-sitting responsibility during Celebrate America!

Nina is four and Eleanor is only two years old — young enough to require *constant* supervision. Nina could ride her two-wheeler with training wheels. But Jessi realized she'd have to push Eleanor in her stroller. She made a mental note to dress in red, white, and blue herself.

Mrs. Marshall liked the plan. "But I won't have time to decorate Nina's bike and the stroller," she told Jessi.

"That's all right," Jessi said. "I'll pick up crepe paper and streamers before I come over in the morning."

"I have about a dozen American flags left over from a July Fourth party," Mrs. Marshall offered. "You could use those."

After Jessi called and told me this, I phoned Logan and asked him if he could help us during Celebrate America! At first he sounded grumpy, as if he didn't want to talk to me about *anything*. But after I told him we were putting the kids in the parade, Logan sounded friendlier. In the end, he came through and said he'd help us. Since my dad was going to work with me, I asked Logan to call Jessi and see what he could do to help her.

When Jessi and I talked on the phone later, she told me that Logan was going to pick up the Braddock kids (and that Becca was going with them instead of her).

We decided to meet in front of the town hall. I spent the next two hours making our signs. It was *very* late when I finally went to bed.

The next morning my group was the first one at the town hall. I saw Kristy's brother Sam riding his unicycle around the town green and motioned to him.

"I don't know how I did it," I told Jessi when she and her group arrived a few minutes later, "but somehow I convinced Sam to let me decorate his unicycle with red, white, and blue crepe paper. And to carry our lead sign."

When I looked around at our fifteen kids, it was hard to believe we'd been so nervous about Celebrate America! All the kids were sticking together and happy about the parade.

And Mr. Braddock videotaped us, which was great because I wanted Kristy to see how Sam looked. He held our lead sign up high as he wove down the street on his unicycle. The sign read:

BSC KIDS ON WHEELS

Our closing signs were pinned to Vanessa's and Becca's shirts. They said:

KEEP THE GOOD   TIMES ROLLING

After the parade, everyone headed to the ballfield for an all-American picnic and some games. The fire department had set up a big barbecue pit and were selling hot dogs (very American) and grilled chicken. There were also potato salad, soda pop, apple pie, and ice cream. What a feast! We put two big picnic tables together for our group and stuck our signs in between them.

After lunch the kids participated in the games and arts-and-crafts activities. The highlights of the afternoon included Jackie Rodowsky winning the sack race and Matt coming in first in an egg-in-spoon race.

But the highlight of the highlights was that so many people sought out Jessi and me to say thank you to the BSC. They weren't just saying thank you for being in the Celebrate America! parade, but for all the good work the BSC does. Even my mother congratulated us, and thanked me for taking care of my brothers and sisters so she could work in the make-your-own kite booth.

That night Jessi and I held a mini-BSC sleepover at her house. We kicked back, relaxed, and celebrated!

CHAPTER 23

Claudia

Saterday
11:30 p.m.

Wat a day! Wat a nikt! I'll never forgit it as long as I live.

Thanks evrybody for all the help with the floot. Sory if I scard you with my costum.

"Today's the parade, today's the parade," Andrew chanted.

"Andrew, you stepped on me," complained Karen.

I opened my eyes and looked around. Karen, Jill, Martha, Dawn, Kristy, and I had all slept on the floor in Mary Anne's room. Andrew was trying, unsuccessfully, to walk between us. He plopped down on my stomach. "Is my mommy home yet?" he asked.

"I don't know," I said. I shifted him off of me so I could get up and look out the window. The only signs of the storm were a couple of broken tree limbs. It was a clear, sunshiny day, perfect for a Founders' Day parade and carnival. But first, I remembered with a shudder, we had to deal with the Coopers — who weren't even really the Coopers. And we couldn't do that until Mr. and Mrs. Menders came home.

I was thinking about the complicated story we had to tell the Menderses when I saw their station wagon pull into the drive. "They're here!" I shouted to the others.

We ran down the stairs and out the front door to greet them, and the Engles.

"Well, well," Mrs. Menders exclaimed. "I've never in my life had such a greeting!"

There was a lot of hugging and kissing and talking about the storm. Then we went into the house for breakfast.

Lionel and Jason announced that they were going to play softball but would be home for lunch and the parade. Before they left, Lionel whispered to me that they wouldn't be part of our float. "We have other plans," he said mysteriously.

Then Jill told her parents that she and Martha were going to a swim team practice, and that they didn't need a baby-sitter. "I can keep an eye on Martha," she explained.

When Kristy was absolutely sure that neither of the Coopers was around, she asked Mr. and Mrs. Menders if we could have a private meeting with them in the front parlor.

When we were all seated, Kristy used her most businesslike tone to start the meeting. "This will come as a shock to you," she began, "but we have evidence that the Coopers aren't who they say they are."

Over the next half hour we laid out all that we'd learned about the Coopers.

We described how they'd tried to convince us and the children that the mansion was haunted.

Kristy told them about what the Coopers planned to do to make life in the mansion miserable — and dangerous — for everyone.

I showed them the photo of their Randolph ancestor and my photocopy of it with the added beard and mustache.

Dawn reported that not only had she heard "Mrs. Cooper" *speak,* but that the woman had a Scottish accent. "So the reason she pretended she couldn't speak," I added, "was because she didn't want anyone to know she was from Scotland."

"Where are the Coop — I mean the Randolphs — now?" Mrs. Menders asked. She looked worried.

"They said they were going to buy groceries," Mary Anne answered.

"Well, that gives us some time to decide how to handle this situation," Mr. Menders said. He looked grim and determined.

"You girls were right not to let on to the Coopers that you suspected them," Mrs. Menders added. "Keep it up a bit longer. Go ahead with the float . . . and have fun. We'll take care of the Coopers."

We stood up. "I'm most grateful to you," Mr. Menders said. "I thought we were engaging baby-sitters. I didn't realize you were detectives, too."

Outside, we found Georgio's truck parked next to the shed. He and Seth were carrying the plywood pieces we'd painted from the shed to the truck. Georgio flashed me a big grin. While we worked on the float I brought Georgio up-to-date on all that had happened during the storm.

It was a fun morning. I liked being with Georgio more than any guy I'd ever been around, and I loved building the float with him.

While we were working, we kept an eye out for the "Coopers," but they didn't show up.

After awhile Mrs. Menders asked Georgio and me to come with her to inspect the "Coopers'" rooms.

It didn't take us long to figure out that the "Coopers" had moved out. Except for the white gown, the drawers and closets were empty.

"They must have known we'd figured out what they were doing," I said. "And that we'd tell you about it."

"Which means you and the kids were in more danger than we realized," Georgio put in.

Mrs. Menders shuddered.

I noticed a piece of spiral notebook paper on the desk. I handed it to Mrs. Menders. "They left you a note," I said. She read it aloud.

The house – and its ghosts –
are yours.
C.R.

"What will happen now?" I asked Mrs. Menders.

"My husband is at the police station. I'll call there with this update. I expect the police will check the airports and see if they can stop the Coopers before they leave the country. But you shouldn't worry about it. We want you to have a fabulous time for the rest of your visit with us. Especially today."

At lunchtime we gathered on the veranda for a make-your-own sandwich meal. Mr. and Mrs. Menders brought out a basket of bread and platters of meats, cheeses, and vegetables. Georgio was invited to eat with us. We were all excited about the parade, but the Menders kids seemed to be the most excited.

When we'd sat down with our sandwiches, Lionel and Jason stood up and simultaneously took off their denim shirts, exposing T-shirts underneath that read *The Locals*.

"It's our team name," Jason said proudly. "Lionel talked the theater into sponsoring us. All the guys on the team have shirts just like these. And we're marching in the parade. We want everyone to know who we are, because we're going to win the championship. Aren't we, Lionel?"

"You bet," Lionel answered.

We cheered. Mr. and Mrs. Menders were smiling proudly at their sons.

After lunch Georgio went to the cottage to clean up and dress for the parade. The rest of us went to our rooms to don our costumes. I waited until I heard everyone else go downstairs before I left my room. Holding up the skirt of the floor-length gown so I wouldn't trip, I climbed the stairs to the fourth floor. Then, using the key Georgio had given me, I opened a door to another shorter flight of stairs. I climbed to the top, opened the door, and stepped out onto the widow's walk. My white satin gown shimmered in the bright sunlight.

The view of the sea from that height was so vast and beautiful it took my breath away. I remembered what the woman at the historical society had told Mary Anne about Mary Randolph. "I expect Mary Randolph grieved for her husband. Perhaps she even took to the widow's walk now and again." And when she did, I thought, she looked out at the sea that killed her husband and became his grave.

I looked toward the ground and saw the

three dimensional replica of the widow's walk that we'd mounted on the pickup truck. Everyone but me was gathered around it.

My friends looked outrageously elegant in their gowns. Kristy had on a red gown and Dawn was in the blue velvet one. Mary Anne wore the yellow gown with the smocking she had admired. The three of them would stand with me on the float.

Georgio was going to drive the float. He was wearing a Union Army uniform. And Andrew — in a sailor suit and carrying the antique toy boat he loved so much — would stand on the float with us baby-sitters. Jill, Martha, and Karen were dressed in party dresses we'd found in an attic trunk. They would walk in front of the float carrying our sign.

I was surprised that no one had discovered me standing on the widow's walk yet. I was about to shout, "Reginald," to get their attention, when Jill looked up and spotted me.

"Look! It's *her*! The ghost!" Jill screamed.

"It's the Claudia ghost!" Dawn yelled.

Everyone was looking up at the widow's walk. I waved. They cheered and waved back.

And that's what being in the parade was like. We waved to the people along the route and they cheered and waved back to us. They loved our sign.

*The Randolph Mansion
wishes Reese a
Happy Birthday!*

After the parade, we returned to the mansion to change from our costumes into the outfits we'd wear for the carnival. Georgio was going to pick me up at seven.

I think I drove Dawn crazy while we were changing. Every time either one of us said something nice about Georgio, I'd add, "Do you think he's too old for me?" Dawn reminded me about her experience with an older guy named Travis. We agreed that Georgio was a lot nicer than Travis, who had thought he could make Dawn over into his idea of what a girlfriend should be. Still, Georgio was *older* than Travis.

During the carnival I successfully put the age difference between me and Georgio out of my mind — at first. We rode the Ferris wheel; tossed rings at bottles; ate hot dogs, french fries, and cotton candy; threw darts; and rode the Ferris wheel again. As we were going up on the Ferris wheel for the second time, I really thought that maybe Georgio could be my boyfriend even though we live hundreds of miles apart. We could write letters, talk on the phone, and visit one another.

Our car stopped at the top. Georgio took

253

my hand in his and said, "Claudia, I'd like you to come to homecoming weekend at my college. It's in October. There's a plane you can take to the airport near school — I already checked. You don't have to answer now. But I want you to promise you'll think about it."

I promised. It wasn't a hard promise to keep. There was a lot to think about. How could I take a plane to Maine to be with a college student for a weekend when I was only thirteen years old? Besides the fact that my parents would never in a hundred million years let me, there was also the fact that Georgio thought I was sixteen!

I thought of Dawn's disastrous fling with Travis. And Stacey's doomed crush on a teacher. But, still, I did love being with Georgio. How could that be wrong?

When the Ferris wheel came to a stop, Mary Anne and Kristy were waiting for us. Kristy said she thought she'd seen Charles Randolph (alias Elton Cooper) near the merry-go-round. "And I think I saw Margaret Cooper," Mary Anne said in a frightened, trembling voice.

"Where did you see her?" I asked Mary Anne.

"Right here. Near the Ferris wheel."

So maybe they hadn't gone away. Maybe they were still in Reese and trying to catch us with our guard down. What if Mrs. Cooper had been trying to interfere with the Ferris wheel to cause an accident? We spent the rest of the night looking for the Coopers at the carnival, and taking turns keeping an eye on the machines that ran the rides.

The mystery might not be over.

EPILOGUE

At breakfast on Sunday morning I found Mrs. Menders and Mary Anne sitting at the table on the veranda. Mr. and Mrs. Menders had been out late the night before, so there hadn't been a chance to tell them about our possible sighting of Margaret Randolph. "Kristy and Dawn are making breakfast," Mary Anne told me. "You and I are on cleanup duty."

I looked over her shoulder and saw that she and Mrs. Menders were making up a schedule of who would do what chores during our last few days in Reese. I was glad to see that they were including Karen and Andrew and the Menders children on the list.

"But this is still vacation," Mrs. Menders said. "Everyone should relax and have fun."

I hated to spoil her mood, but I had to tell her that we thought we'd seen Charles Randolph and his wife at the carnival.

Mrs. Menders told me that I must have been mistaken. "Charles and Margaret Randolph are already back in Scotland," she said. "We just received a call from the police saying the Randolphs left the country on a late flight from Boston."

"What are you going to do about them?" I asked.

"We may not do anything," Mrs. Menders answered. "There aren't really any charges we can file. Unless they bother us again."

We had a ball those last few days in Reese. With the adults around more, and the Menders kids taking care of one another, there were long stretches of time when we sitters didn't have even one kid to sit for. That left plenty of time for a thorough search of the attic for the treasure.

We didn't find a chest of gold coins and jewels. So we told the Menderses the story of what Mr. Menders's uncle had said on his deathbed about the treasure in his attic.

"I think we have a big enough treasure in inheriting this wonderful property as our home," Mr. Menders said. "Perhaps that's what Uncle Randolph meant. That the estate was his treasure and he wished he could take it with him in death."

I thought that was an interesting idea, but I wasn't sure I agreed. I had this nagging feeling there was a treasure we'd missed. I told myself that I shouldn't expect to solve the "Mystery of the Hidden Treasure," but be satisfied that we'd survived, and solved, the "Mystery of the Haunted House."

Dear Claudia:

You've been gone a day and I miss you already. I only spent ten days with you, so why does it feel like I've known you all my life?

The Menders kids are doing great. Everyone is happy that the "Coopers" are gone, including yours truly.

I'm counting on seeing you on homecoming weekend. We'll have a terrific time. There's a rock concert, a clambake on the beach, and of course a big dance. But October's so far away. Let's find a way to be together before that.

I have to go to work now, but will write a longer letter soon.

Here are some petals from <u>our</u> rose garden.

Love,
Georgio

Dear Georgio:

Thanks a lot for your great letter. I miss seeing you every day. I have something important to tell you. I'm thirteen years old. When you guessed I was sixteen I didn't tell you the truth. I'm sorry. I know you said you have friends all different ages. But six years is just too big a difference between us. For example, I can't go to homecoming weekend. My parents wouldn't let me. Besides, I'd feel out of place with all those college students.

Maybe when we're both older six years won't be such a big deal. Meanwhile, I hope I can be one of your friends who happens to be a girl.

Please write again soon.

Claudia

P.S.
I had a wonderful time with you in Reese, especially at the carnival.

Dear Becca,
I know I've been a lousy big sister to you lately. I feel awful about it. I'm really sorry. Will you forgive

me? I say it's
time to do some
serious Rollerblading.
How about it?
                Love,
                Jessi

    I OU 5 hours of
Rollerblade Instruction

Dear Dawn, Kristy, Claudia,
and Mary Anne,
    Thank you for taking
care of us. I like being
a baby-sitter, too. Georgio
found me a job as a
mother's helper. I help
Mrs. Johnson take care of
Tammy. Tammy's four.
Sometimes. Martha
helps me babysit for
Tammy. I told Martha
she could be a junior
member of my baby-sitting
club. Is that okay?
        Your friend and
        fellow baby-sitter,
        Jillian Menders

260

Dear Sitters:

Are you sitting down? You better be because I have big news. I got a small (but not too small) role in Our Town. Yes, I, Lionel, the pain-in-the-neck guy who complained that there was nothing to do in Reese. Now I'm complaining there's too much to do in Reese. I told my parents I have to go back to Boston for a rest.

Anyway, thanks for helping us city kids learn to like life in a small town.

Lionel

DEAR KRISTY:

YOU'RE A GOOD SOFTBALL PLAYER FOR A GIRL. THANK YOU FOR HELPING ME MAKE A TEAM. WE WON OUR FIRST GAME 10 TO 7. EVERYONE IN THE REC ROOM SAYS HI. IT STOPPED RAINING SO WE CAN PRACTICE NOW. GOTTA GO.

JASON

DEAR MARTHA:

HOW ARE YOU? HAVE YOU MADE ANY NEW FRIENDS LATELY? HOW IS THE SWIM TEAM? I HAD A GOOD TIME AT YOUR HOUSE. BEING IN THE PARADE WAS THE BEST. CAN YOU COME VISIT ME? I HAVE LOTS OF FRIENDS THAT YOU WOULD LOVE TO MEET. I WILL HAVE A BIG PARTY FOR YOU.

YOUR FRIEND,
KAREN

261

Dear Karen:

I have three new friends in Reese. If you were here we could have a party. My swim team is doing good. I win a lot of ribbons.

Your friend,
Martha

Dear Claudia:

How are you? We enjoyed your visits very much. I am writing to tell you what's happened to us since you left. At Georgio's suggestion we had tea at the mansion with Mr. and Mrs. Menders. As you may have heard, their caretaker couple left them quite suddenly. Mr. and Mrs. Menders asked us if we would like to come out of retirement and work part time for them. The next day Georgio helped us move back into our little house by the pond. I am writing this note in my garden.

Our warm regards to you and the other members of your club. I learned all about it from Jill while we were baking.

Sincerely,
Bertha Tiono

DEAR MR. AND MRS. MENDERS:
I HAD A GOOD TIME AT
YOUR HOUSE. YOUR HOUSE
IS BIG. THANK YOU FOR GIVING
ME THE BOAT. KRISTY AND ME
CLEANED IT. THERE WAS
WRITING ON THE SIDE. IT
SAID, "TREASURE." KRISTY
SAID TO TELL YOU, " THE
BOAT WAS THE TREASURE IN
THE ATTIC."
                    ANDREW

P.S. KRISTY HELPED ME WRITE
THIS LETTER. SHE SAYS, HI!

When our Reese vacation was over, I still had to write my summer composition for Mrs. Hall. I reread our Reese notebook and thought about how to organize all that had happened to us in Reese. In those ten days I had acquired an awful lot to write about.

I decided to start at the beginning, with our first night in the Randolph mansion, and then to let the story unfold. I was nervous before I started writing, but once I began it was easier than I had thought it would be. I typed the second draft of my paper on Janine's computer and used the spellcheck. Then I gave my paper a title — THE MYSTERY OF THE HAUNTED HOUSE — included my drawings of the mansion, and turned it in.

Guess what? I got an A!

About the Author

ANN M. MARTIN did *a lot* of baby-sitting when she was growing up in Princeton, New Jersey. She is a former editor of books for children, and was graduated from Smith College.

Ms. Martin lives in New York City with her cats, Mouse and Rosie. She likes ice cream and *I Love Lucy*; and she hates to cook.

Ann Martin's Apple Paperbacks include *Yours Turly, Shirley*; *Ten Kids, No Pets*; *With You and Without You*; *Bummer Summer*; and all the other books in the Baby-sitters Club series.